PUNK
BLOOD

PUNK BLOOD

JAY MARVIN

Published by FC2
with support given by The English Department
Unit for Contemporary Literature of Illinois State University
and the Illinois Arts Council

This work originally appeared in a slightly different form
on floppy disc from Spectrum Press, Chicago.

Address all inquiries to:
FC2
Unit for Contemporary Literature
Campus Box 4241
Illinois State University
Normal, IL 61790-4241

ISBN: 1-57366-047-7 (paperback)

**Library of Congress Cataloging Number
98-071787**

Book Design: Michele Steinbacher-Kemp
Cover Design: Todd Michael Bushman

Produced and Printed in the United States of America

Acknowledgments

Thanks to Edward Bunker and Bill Shields who lived through it all and wrote about it. Thanks to Ronald Sukenick, Dan Agin, Tom Russell, Claude Simon, Samuel Beckett, Che Guevara, all the small time punks and thieves I have known, to Donna and Fred—Cop Friends to the end, and to Mary who lives with it all with much love.

Hard driving all night cactus and sand smell of unleaded gasoline topped off under long rows of bright fluorescent light driving moths and earwigs mad in the desert night I drive on hungry for the stars white hot candies in a licorice sky you could reach out and scoop them up crumpled pack of smokes on the dashboard white bursts of static and country music guitar brown clashing and fighting the sounds of L.A. sea green surf tunes sets of headlights side by side planets rolling towards me red lights like hot pokers retreating into luminous black ink lead foot it deeper into the flat night road signs yell split pea soup in loud greens and cheap lodging twenty five miles up the road giant hot dogs thick shakes made from dates and figs in fat yellows won't you have some now I have no appetite thanks to the rush of the rip off soaking my cells pushing me onward making my brain jump and flip like a pair of black jumper cables hooked to my fucking head the car grinding metal against metal my head grinding cell against cell bone against bone my throat and nose coated in brown tar I take a hit from a bottle of shit brand whiskey to try and take the edge off it was so bad at the last gas up I almost wasted the fucking attendant my hands shaking trying to top off the tank the handle to the gas pump like a gun the barrel a gentle toxic arc probing and crashing into the side of the car trying to connect with the opening for the fuel piloted by shaky hands gripping tight racked by tremors like hot sparks drops of gas spilling on the slick oiled pavement then as if he were a blind man finding the stepping off point from a curb the gun finds its way into the opening hands white knuckled pulling up on the nozzle's trigger filling the tank I sign one of the many stolen credit cards boosted from a B & E off Sunset Boulevard there's always ten or twelve seconds when you think the computer is going to rat you out and there's no way you'll do time for it so then things get ugly and you're not in the mood for the shit and thank God it didn't happen because the car you're in is hot and you're hot and tonight you have to get off the fucking road and lay low dreams of TV and a lumpy bed run through your head I fight a spasm of pain in my neck pull into a rest area unfold a map like tattered soda crackers and try and figure out how the hell I'm going to get to Mexico before they find me and bust me for the cash I boosted in broad daylight at a small savings and loan I took down in the Valley I shake my head trying to throw off the fatigue the way a dog sheds water its paralyzing hands on me trying to jerk me off the road a grand battle exhaustion versus the fading adrenaline going on in my skull this isn't the first time I've scrambled down the white line like a spider wanting cover its hairy rubber legs probing for darkness and safety and it may be the last time unless I get clear and settle down the fucking action in a nameless flop false dead light because there's no way I can put it down in a high profile name brand right off the interstate instead I have to find a flop where no one will ask any questions and no one will run any plates the man behind the desk to busy jerking off to girlie mags pink flesh and high gloss bodies check you right in no candy red Caddies and simulated wood station wagons oh boy the kids get to eat for free how far to Las Vegas and what do you know about Circus Circus kiddy time reds and yellows with balloons and bull shit not what I need or want ignoring the roadside billboards one right after another wouldn't be in this shape if it hadn't been for my own fucking greed failing to notice the rent a cop behind me I panicked and opened up killing the fake cop and three others what use does it serve to go back over it now nothing will change and it will only cloud my head cause me to fuck up give myself away if I'm going to do that why not call the boys in blue right now tell them and the Feds where I am win a free trip to the g chamber listen to the pellets drop strapped down fighting for air jerking and struggling to keep from growing wings I don't think so I yell out loud passing

mile marker after mile marker eyes poached egg white and
paprika red searching for a place to shut it down for the night
don't know how much longer I can keep at it blown all over
the fucking road by these big rigs my only cover the night I
keep the speed down to the double nickel creeping and crawling in and around the various big semi's like a high powered
reddish black cockroach trying to stay out of the kitchen light
I pass a couple of cop cars parked on the shoulder asleep like
sharks bellies full of fenders tires and vin numbers they stay
put I move on five miles outside Tarantula Gulch Arizona the
other side of the canyon the Golden State my eyes lock on a
small motel the El Mesa Traveler and I steer the car into the lot
to check in the office so bright it hurts my pickled egg eyes a
small TV spits out an old western in blue gray splashes a cheap
plastic white desk fan sweeps the area like a giant rubber
radar unit the room smells of stale smoke and disinfectant the
desk clerk is a large man stacked brown beef hung on large
shoulders like a close rack his yellowish nubby fingers takes
the cash I pay in S&L money not a great idea can't use hot
cards here he'll run the account overnight and rat me out he
gives me the key attached to a reddish oval piece of plastic
worn gold lettering on it I avoid eye contact keep my head
down and go right to my room for a dime I'd waste his fucking
big ass the large man sits in the swivel chair behind the motel
desk white shirt and bolo tie black hair slicked back flat nose
and small eyes the other man tall eyes like flamed burnt char-
coal pulls a gun from his waist and lashes out at the large ham
behind the desk spraying blood and smashing his nose the big
man tries to get up and the other man strikes him again leaving a large gash on the side of the big man's head he collapses
back in the chair and the tall man fires two shots driving the
large man's head back like a kiddy ride a small river of sticky
red liquid seeps from a dark hole below the scalp the air conditioner starts with a rumble and I try and sack out visions of
the road white lines rolling past my eyes pouring over my
head still behind the wheel the last traces of electricity dancing out of my body I pull out a bottle lay it on the bed set my
gun down and a small baggy of uppers and downers their
multi colors like sweet candy you tried to steal from a jar of
treats when you were a kid clothes off I lay in bed calling for
sleep its not in the neighborhood all I can do is toss and turn
black and white outlines illustrating the events of the last twenty

four hours in then out the cash in a bag running to the car sounds of sirens the car engine wide open raw the dead left on the expensive marble floor a cold slab to go out on the jolt of pulling the fucking trigger sounds of rounds going off shells dropping on the floor I lay on the bed the air conditioner fucked up burned out box sticking out the window speaks to me in mechanical language like a broken record whispering death over and over again a tin voice I can't get out of my brain until I want to rip the fucking thing from the wall and smash it to pieces easy I tell myself you don't need it right now the booze and fatigue doing to much talking I take another gulp of whiskey stumbling around the room bottle in hand like an old man with a divining rod searching for water praying for sleep flipping TV channels the gun and the bottle laughing at me their thin voices bouncing off my skull the way faces appear if you stare at a stucco wall long enough the odd eyes and noses coming and going with the crawling of the brain like a squid moving along the ocean floor the quiet of the desert starts to eat at my guts in small flesh ripping bites I take another shot from the hard wagon it does nothing to kill the constant swimming of drink and drugs through my spider capillaries the ticking goes on a giant clock in my head white and black calling off the seconds I sit on the bed and light a smoke how long have those stupid people in the S&L been dead now time melts moves and stands still in the false light and continuous prattling of the air conditioner it seems so very far away yet so close like time has lurched forward then stopped and now is going forward like globs of liquid mercury rolling around on a table top I'm grungy from head to toe a fine oil of criminal craziness coating my body I check out the shower stall coated with mold green and rust orange the curtains cheap plastic brown along the edges I long for a cold barrage the water soothing in its chill but I don't want to be pinched bare ass in the shower and who knows when the blue boys and the Feds will come for me if at all who am I fooling they always come for you one way or another it's a game the outcome assured I lay back on the bed letting the bottle ride on the sea of my belly the sick television picture amplified and twisted through the liquid in the amber bottle is this what a person's last moments are like when he's alone and ready to cross to the other side from light to dark he gets off the bed and slowly picks the gun up off the table frees the

safety catch and gently shoves the gun's barrel up against the
roof of his mouth there's laughter seeping out of the walls his
finger sweaty on the trigger one pull and he'll be free to whirl
in the darkness move in the quiet one pull is all it takes the
laughter grows louder he sees himself doing it over and over
he wants to make the journey from one hell to another he
thinks about his soul softly floating over the desert's surface
his life a flood of memories like the first time he popped his
cherry a used car parts scam he and bunch of others stole a
1948 pickup truck and drove it around ripping out car radiators smell of rubber weakened by heat on his hands and hub
caps chipping his finger nails prying them off Caddies Lincolns
and Jags the truck piled high with greasy parts and tape play-
ers wires red and black spaghetti running out the back of black
box shells they weren't getting rich it was enough to score and
get high hemp burning their young thug throats laughing their
asses off at the stiffs who would get up the next morning to
find their cars had no radiators or were missing batteries the
acid once spilling on his hands Christ it burned like a wielder's
torch a million steel spikes boring into the bones nothing to
do but drive around like a drug beaten dog searching for water the chemical heating up his skin what sweet Colorado River
relief from a garden hose the next time he stole a pair of his
mother's green and white rubber house gloves menial colored
to handle the black rubber blocks DC current and it went on
through the summer and half of the fall until one night he saw
it sitting like a slick painted shark its black and white calling
out to him in a voice he couldn't turn down those lights red
and blue the power of that engine and the sound of its siren
he tried jimmying open the driver's side door before he could
get the metal door cracked open he felt a dull prodding against
his back an officer's gun cold steel head shoved down in the
backseat handcuffed at the station he was met by his parents
tears in his mother's eyes how were they going to explain this
to the crowd at the synagogue he didn't care and went home
listening to the two of them scream while he looked out the
car window planning how he was going to get the fuck out or
kill them both it wasn't until he was seventeen that he got that
ride in a police car the way he wanted it stealing one at Denny's
parking lot on Tustin Avenue picking up his sweet moist open
girlfriend Nash short for Nassau and they drove the squad car
to an orange grove off Irvine road and fucked her feet up

against the dashboard kicking the siren on and off and playing with the radio Nash getting on and asking cops if they wanted their cocks sucked to a chorus of laughter and clicks the trees and leaves laughing and swaying green fragrant in the slow breeze when the cops found the car they were gone it was a gas reading about it the next day in the Times checking the paper there's nothing about the robbery and the dead and I don't know why I'm looking for it except it beats clawing the skin off my face now bathed in sweat and grime I still have the bag of cash and no I shouldn't go for anymore meth or booze so I suck down more whiskey anyway and pop some downers because I'm either going to get fucking smashed out of my prow or I'm going to snort the rest of that sexy power powder and rip me another set of wheels and head deeper into the desert bugs and night creatures all over the wind-shield like downed airplanes and the sound of clear air pushing past the car window elbow hanging out and this makes me even sadder and madder because I know if I get out there I'll get busted the TV set playing an old black and white movie I try to watch it and can't like when I was in high school English class couldn't dig poetry and all that Shakespeare shit only thing I wanted to do was rape my English teacher she was blonde and cute her legs so choice made by the Devil's right hand every guy wanted her and I wanted her bad following her home one night and peeking in her window the woman's shocking white skin set against her male lover's legs thrust in the air feet splayed her hands grasping at the man's back tear-ing at his flesh outside at the window he knelt on his knees and freed his stiff cock the head purple and swollen sitting listening to the sounds of the two lovers he started to stroke the shaft she was nude wrapped in the arms of her spouse they rolled on the bed and he sat there on his haunches mouth dry blood on fire pulse banging in his ears her smooth pale skin against his tan muscular body and his head buried in her blond thatch between her legs of the three of them he got off first covering the sounds he wanted to make staying to check the end of the show the next day looking at her in class it drove him crazy he broke in her house it was the first B&E job he had ever pulled and stole a handful of her panties to jack off on and cash to spend on booze and drugs never getting caught it started a streak of luck and it taught him a lesson the short jobs were to be his meat and not big boosts the way some guys did it and when most were heading off to state sponsored higher learning he was getting higher putting meth and coke up his nose God you could steal a car like a slick fox the meth sawing through your veins and power lifting your fucking head to the hem of Jesus in the manger I sit down on the edge of the bed and finger the gun thinking I should blow my head off right now I put the barrel against my right temple its cold circular edge digging into my scalp like a big period at the end of a long sentence and I pull the trigger it clicks and nothing happens my hand shaking I drop the gun vomit all over the bed every thing moving back and forth at once trying to get my God damn shit together I lay in the foul liquid unable to move what the fuck is going on here the TV continues to spew out useless programming beamed from the first big city this side of the Cal State line into the desert night nothing for miles the cactus and rocks fed endless jitter and jive about used car parts and face creams I want to pull myself off the bed and smash the mother fucking set kill it like its killing me rolling out crap and noise man when was the last time you could shut everything off including your own mind and float in the silence its something that never happens even if you can close out the world you can never shut your God damn head off I know I've been at it for years and I know I've got to get over thinking about this they only have a vague description at best on who pulled the job and how are they going to find out no one saw me and no one cares so color the four assholes history the streak is there man why fight it why this constant crawling out on the fucking edge daring yourself to go over I take another shot from the bad news bottle trying to get the sour taste of bile out of my fucking mouth and now when I look back I've been this way most of my life example I pull into a liquor store to score a pint and the stem behind the counter doesn't look right and he's getting on my fucking nerves talk talk talk I pulled out my nine and pistol whipped the mother fucker into dreamland and rifle the cash drawer no casing the joint no nothing feeling good about it the power to fuck over some stupid ugly person who has no reason to even get a hard on why I didn't get caught who knows the guy's bloods splattered all over the glass case copper red drops on the floor his bowels letting loose he pisses all over himself in a stinking yellow stream so I got even madder and kicked him twenty times until I couldn't catch my breath staggering from the store like a an over weight man suffering from a massive coronary I fucked her until I passed out the smell of her dark brown muff on my lips and mouth or I would walk with a pronounced limp and gain the confidence of an elderly person they always made the best marks and hustle them off to the back of a store or alley and bitch slap them until they gave it up even broke one old lady's arm the bone snapping like a fresh a cold orange carrot I left her screaming the arm dangling out of its socket as I hot footed it down the alley into the passing crowd lucky once again I didn't get picked up living in a dump and driving a set of trashed out wheels unless I decided to go out and hot-wire another one for a little joy ride around the old town playing chicken with the black and whites in a stolen car and once I left a car parked in my parents' driveway I knew my father the old fuck was shitting a square one out to get the paper in the morning and here's this hot sled nesting in his drive I laughed my ass off for weeks over that deal nothing on TV so I try the radio static and Tex Mex music all news KNX out of L.A. nothing on the Valley job why wasn't it good enough to make the big time I can feel the rage coming up hot red and white gut string pulled tight didn't even make the news Christ I iced four people what the fuck one in the morning walk the floor psychotic bull shit I sit on the bed and count the squares on the rug and check the worn spots trying to add them up in my head anything to shut it off and stop the whole fucking mess from driving me out of my mind the first thing he can remember from his childhood nothing but a baby staring at the squares on the carpet his body is drawn towards a small box encrusted in jewels reds and blues purples bright shiny colors he senses his body move towards the box like he had no control over it wasn't until years later he figured out what it was and where he was two women's legs and high heeled shoes in front of him his mother and another woman smart boy he was into boosting the goods back then almost sexual thrill feel to it like having to take a piss holding it the tingle climbing the skin same jolt he gets from doing crimes and killing the pain inside the raw meat of his stomach standing at a urinal his real father there both of them arching a stream the older man showing the young child how grownup men go to the bathroom the two of them standing there he loved him the most until he walked out of his life at age four never could figure out what happened to him walk-

ing through life shell shocked sitting in first grade having to
shit scared to ask where to go he passed gas so loud the other
children laughed the teacher Japanese coming up to him and
asking if he had a problem it was the first time he had seen a
person with almond eyes the small disruptions on her skin
matched the small bubbles from his own gas was illustrated
right before him he was excused to go and instead ran from
school wandering the streets until afternoon getting a whip-
ping from his mother's new hubby him and her a belt in each
of their hands he cried and wanted dad he was gone and later
he found out his old man was a fag out on Sunset Boulevard
getting his cock sucked while he lived in this strange house
with people he hated he only hoped the blow jobs were worth
it I stare at my hands and wonder how much of the skin cells
have been through it with me and how many have fallen off
and died like those I ran with and did crimes with playing the
old road games and maybe that's what I should do call some
fuckers back in L.A. and see if the heats out the bunch of them
standing around on street corners on the hunt for crystal better than sugar trying to cop without getting taken down I know
I can't call there are no friends some dirt bag would snitch on
me sure as I'd beat the shit out of an old lady out for a Sunday
morning walk I take another glance at the time it's only fucking
ten after one the bottle almost gone and no sleep what the
fuck do I do now I unzip my pants and prod and pull on my
cock trying to jack off to the images of a dumb cunt I met
weeks before in the Bull Pen Lounge downtown off Spring
Street sour memory music on the box never sounding right
always going slower than it should the horn sections sounding
like syrup poured from a cold bottle blue and yellow half lit
liquid beer signs a small crowd of beaten men and women
hugging the long wooden bar her long legs and pixie nose he
figured her for a working muff copping a squat because if she
was hustling it on the street there was no money here so they
talked and drank and in an alley behind the joint hip deep in
trash and rats the rain beating down on both of them in long
gray sheets she got down on her knees and did him right there
his head turned towards the angry sky deciding then and there
he would use this sweet dumb bitch for a setup a sting big
bold and befitting a good angle to run around town net some
cash and roll like he always wanted to could he love this gash
her worn scuffed high heels and chipped red nails she always

chewed on the left corner of her thumb when he talked to her no he couldn't he had never known love his heart cold empty like the stone on a roadside picnic table in Montana in February his brain like a dead tray of meat set out to rot in the sun every time he took a breath he was playing a sick game he would never win a puzzle and someone else held all the parts so he could only fuck her and work her and then drop her when he didn't need her anymore but for now out she went tricking for bucks for junk and rent and she would go into another's arms for the flash of green and one night he watched like his English teacher all over again only this time it made him grow even colder and he went out and beat up a punk with an orange Mohawk off Sunset and Vaness his fingers in the kid's mouth and thumbs pushing in on his eyeballs blood on a brick wall his chest pumping like a machine his victim's stomach soft like a lump of dough he had thirty-eight dollars pushed inside dirt crusted leather pants he left him there on the street sure the angels would prep him up fine but he lived he read it in the Times the next day and before he was done he had scored sweet and burned his nose good came back to the flop and he fucked her again and again going where others had been at first she said no and he said I'm going to do you until it's red worn out fucking her until he thought his heart was going to blow out and she trying to make him think she dug what was up and he slapped her across the face stop fucking faking it I'm not honey she cried and he hit her again and jammed his speed driven cock into her face if you can't do better that then get the fuck out you no good cunt he yelled they rolled on the bed and floor and in the end he thought he was going to die couldn't catch his breath she trying to help him and him feeling a tinge of guilt never deviating from his central plan of mind and body all will pay for God putting me on this fucking earth he yelled and gulped a bunch of downers chased with whiskey crashed out she by his side bloody mouth worn vagina red in pain later he wondered why she didn't kill him when she had the chance maybe he was the only one of the two of them who could kill cold and not think about it twice rob and not think about it twice I picked up the empty bottle and hefted in my hand I wanted to had to and did throwing it against the wall it shattered and I got up and peaked out the motel window nothing a few parked cars and a big rig red and box like how about if I jack that baby not cool got to lay low try not to count the hours until sun up then move to a better spot shit this hole could use paint the walls worn and grimy on the edges and near the ceiling I wonder how many people have fucked in this room how many fights bouts of sickness besides the ultimate sickness which only I carry the sickness to destroy to hate and to hurt to steal I never wanted to be this way always the one standing in the rain looking in on the sunshine if I live past this maybe I'll rehab tried it once couldn't fucking cut it got to stop going over the same ground again and again like a plowed out field the bits of logic drifting in the dry wind like spent dirt they pulled jobs and cons and road games over Southern California playing Drunken Sailor in Pedro she hooking them and luring them into an alley and he hitting them with a bat and cleaning them out he snatched most of the cash she got some they blasted together right or wrong was never an issue for those two only survival mostly his survival always moving forward like a shark maybe that's why I can't sleep I've done the big one and there's no going back now it's beyond right or wrong I keep playing with this let's spit out the truth it's the fear of death and punishment and confinement he saw a small child standing on the sidewalk a dirty chocolate smudged face and a grimy quarter in its hand he needed a quarter for a phone call the child slowly opened its small hand and held the coin for him to see as if to say look what I have and he reached down without even thinking and took the quarter the child started to cry and tried to hold onto him he pushed the kid away and the tot screamed and it ran back into a nearby park and he made the phone call never thinking twice of right or wrong of it amoral to the last fucking cell I'm lying I do know what right from wrong is I always packed it away into a wall in my head and left it there like hiding a dead body the flesh falling from the frame a rotting corpse stuffed in a crawl space wrapped in thick gauze or sunk deep in murky water the glint off the minerals reflecting up letting you know the dangers of sticking your arms into the shit slime up to your elbows pull-ing out your rights and wrongs and examining them until it eats you alive like a creature biting down and biting down again to tear at your skin hungry for understanding and thirsty for forgiveness I never wanted any part of that shit the kind of shit kings and heads of state the big guys are always telling us little fry about right and wrong fuck them and up their God damn holes everyone of them your parents going to tell you what the fuck to do I'll write my own rules thank you it's not my fault the fucking rules are defined early in life offering choice A which is to kiss ass all your life and maybe end up in a trailer watching some worn out whore grow old with you or B getting out there and getting what you need while you can still need and want and spend because if it's early or late your going to head out feet first and you can't stuff it in your mouth laying dead on a slab headed for an unmarked grave fucking zero so sitting around waiting for sorrow to set in is a waste of time now it is setting in with me Christ I should pull the trigger I won't and can't it's a matter of principle I killed four fucking people make that five if you count her the fucking lying cheating hole and I'm going to beat this one like every other one so if I have to sit here in this room TV going letting my mind work like a pulse in the ugliness of what I've become so be it I have no more to drink the drug is wearing thin my body aches for sleep and peace yet if I close an eye and they get on to me they'll take me like a docile animal without a struggle yes when it came to the final moment of truth Marvin Cohen Jew boy petty criminal accused murderer stick up man walked out of his motel room hands up without as much as a shot fired one bystander was quoted as saying he looked like a nice young man to me well fuck you Pops you're only about a thousand years old and what the fuck are you doing in a dump like this anyway oh on vacation with the Misses of 50 years huh got a nice car there Pops got any bread in those pockets and if so hand it over or I'll jack your head so hard your teeth will turn to dust and the worms will nest in your eye sockets there I go again can't turn off that voice no bottle only the bag I can't touch have to have discipline need it in the morning going to drive to the other end of North America in three nights because they have no leads and no one will talk because no one saw me kill her and I never noticed if anyone saw me leave the federally guaranteed institution I'll be in some foreign country snug and safe and it won't take me long to figure out how to get it done a collection of stolen credit cards spent at strategic locations and you could live for a long time before they'd even be able to track you down and hook the wires up to your shaved head and turn on the juice they say your head jerks back and forth and smoke curls up around your skull the stench of human flesh permeates the chamber exhaust fans on full to suck the sickening smell out of the small steel space flat iron or shiny I'll bet you the paint is chipped along the order of green or gray bolts like the belly of a ship rust around the bolts form the humidity of human misery and when it's done your soul is sucked out the exhaust and into the atmosphere so it can hover above the scene of the execution before taking its ride into red hot hell they came to his cell close to midnight and shaved his head and legs barefooted they led him to a tiny holding cell his last meal greasy tacos and a lump of refried beans dabbed with sour cream he ate none of it just sat and smoked angry like a twisted pit bull they sent a rabbi in to see him and he told the old man to take his Bible and prayer shawl and fuck off he would meet God the same way he had met life alone and with no special help from anyone when it was over he had said nothing to anyone leaving the guards who had watched him in his final hours shaken sure he was hanging from the Devil's pitch fork right now I light a smoke and turn back to the TV my only companion sitting there glowing in the middle of the night throwing off daggers of blues blacks and greens ripping with static some kind of murder movie the small speaker webbed with cheap brown and gold netting the material makes me want to reach in and pull out the paper and tar and wiring from the black speaker cone like when I use to tear up old radios parts lying everywhere Christ I didn't know they still had sets with knobs for tuners and corrugated cardboard ventilated backs screwed to the rear of the set I lean forward and twist the volume knob the sound crackles making a white noise like pieces of sand paper rubbed together the movie brought to you by Rockin' Bob Barry's 24 hour Ford Chrysler Plymouth plant where you need no credit ninety days same as cash a parade of late model cars move across the screen drops of rain dot the hoods like tiny clear beads made bright by false light the screen blacks out and then lights the credits roll down the glass display in white frosting I move close to the set pull up a chair near the edge of the bed leaning in to fine tune the baby the picture jumps and gets a big dose of hash before settling down and clearing up I let my head eat into the picture an electronic narcotic sucking me away from my own preoccupations the phone rings I'm jarred awake causing my head to jerk like I've been rear ended who the hell would call at this time of night I grab for the phone it falls to the floor I hear a

21

voice shouting hello hello I stumble around like a psychotic mine sweeper lost in a heavy fog a thousand miles gone gray in the middle of nowhere down on all fours I try to follow the voice flashes of audio rising and fading the texture of the greasy carpet under my hands I pick the phone up and listen something about a murder out in the Valley girl stuffed in a trash can why this time of night yes I'll get over there right away I turn on the light on the floor big black letters splashed on newsprint jump out at me late model Fords and Chryslers the dealership is Rockin' Bob Barry it's the car guy who's plastered on TV I stumble to the bathroom run a toothbrush over my mossy teeth I hate the taste of toothpaste and step into a lukewarm shower thousands of beads of water run down my back tiny bits of liquid buckshot disrupting my skin and pushing my blood trying to drive me awake the smell of soap bites at my nose and reminds of the Proctor and Gamble plant off U.S. 101 I always wondered what it would be like to work there men dressed in heavy white coats and overalls hands covered by green rubber gloves moving vats of white soap and whale fat the fumes clean to the consumer's nose become toxic and nauseating to the worker tiny bars machine wrapped in non-loving care clocking out at the end of the day home to a white refrigerator and four burner gas stove two kids and a tender wife in pants and blouse girl like red hair reading Movie Time kids with tow heads and shiny teeth jeans rolled in cuffs a smudge of dirt on one of the Childs' right cheeks and knees grass-stained a nice roast for dinner and the evening newspaper until TV time when the whole family gathers around for their favorite show I step out in the cold dry myself off and dress the smell of fresh socks making me feel even worse my whole body off schedule I know I'll not only be tired but sick to my stomach for the rest of the day the car is cold and doesn't want to start the radio glaring and hissing at me in the dark the sounds of surf music mixed with rapid fire Spanish I turn the key the electrical system strains to turn the engine over sucking electricity from the radio it goes dark and then glows and squawks again the engine popping and struggling on its mounts trying to work free I give it more gas and it races the smell of cold motor oil and gas fumes filling the car reminds me of the blue and white Arco sign I open the door and try and vomit a lump in my throat it has to go one way or the other I score a soft drink from an all night store the sweet dark syrup and bubbles clear my throat and soothe my stomach I back out onto the vacant street lamps bright in dead white glow on the way to the crime scene well-manicured lawns reinforce the demand for order and compliance giving one a feeling of comfort knowing everything appears as it should even if it may not be how many women took it on the chin in those houses last night what does it matter as long as the bodies are not seen and only heard Mr. and Mrs. Soap Worker won't give a damn what's out there and what's happening until they're at the door kicking it in guns everywhere a tall man in a ski mask grabs one of the children and rams his head into the wall laughing the Childs' father tries to help but is struck hard by a second man in a Bill Clinton Mask the features smooth wax like the father drops to his knees and the man with Clinton's face kicks him in the head his teeth scatter on the floor like loose thumb tacks the two men then point shotguns at the mother and her daughter push them against a corner wall in the background ex- presidential candidate Pat Robertson is grinning and talking on the TV the one with the hood yanks down the mother's dress and slaps her twice then pulls out his huge dick and puts it in her face and yells suck it bitch suck it the mother is crying and the daughter watches while the mother works it the rest of the family watches her lips and mouth handle the foreign object then she is forced to start on the second man both men laughing guns sneering and prowling the air when she is done they zip up and fill pillow cases full of items of value and start for the door before they make their exit the daughter gets to her feet and cries no wait and then in a soft voice like a child asking for an ice cream she mumbles take me with you no the mother yells Cynthia what are you doing take me with you the daughter asks again the man in the Clinton mask extends his hand she takes it and they make for the door another Democrat another Union man gone Republican his wife sobbing and bleeding father left in a daze I see it all the time get tough on law and order the world safe for no one welcome to America I pull up to the crime scene police vehicles everywhere lights pounding blue and red early morning dew coats the world in damp sorrow another soul taken from life space the only thing left an image in someone's mind of an encounter in a motel room or alley bleach blond skull down on its knees or on all fours drugs and guns now a cheap casket in a pile of dirt somewhere unless claimed by grieving relatives from North Dakota she was such a good girl right out of a crime novel no one is good she sucked so many cocks and shot so many drugs she couldn't tell one from the other we'll get the bastard who killed your child I'll bet my shield on it I have the whole speech in my head ready for use if and when the lab boys do their work I lean up against the hood of the car light a smoke and feel the heat coming off the metallic surface eventually the heat will dissipate because everything comes to an end sooner or later I watch bodies move in shades of black and blue uniforms and non-uniforms swarming over the scene my hand reaches down and touches the car's headlights they're small and foreign looking steel rims around the glass covers small e-x on the front of the hood it's funny how man-made things can outlive the maker where are the men and women who built this car and what are they doing now and who will go first will they or will the metal from this car be melted down and used for something else or will both end up in a graveyard of sorts the car in a yard somewhere rusting away eaten little by little by the weather and the people who made it six feet under alienated from the product they produced I get up from the bed and light a smoke and search the drawers of the room cheap furniture cigarette burns and coffee mug rings makes me want to puke the TV rattles away grappling with the sound of the air conditioner this goddamn stinking hell-hole a small pool of brown water gathered in a sick puddle under the air conditioner causing the carpet to buckle and smell how long has it been since I've had anything to eat the drug and booze closing down my desire for food even though its been reduced now to an almost quiet low buzzing wave white and purring I'm not about to go out now and get anything hi there officer what am I doing with this hot box of shit on wheels well you see I smoked this two bit fucking chippy and I needed the wheels to escape in I go to the sink in the bathroom and take a drink of water the fluid drying up as soon as it meets the skin of my throat the way water beads up on a waxed surface the tar from endless cigarettes clinging to the back of my teeth I sit down on the bed the picture on the TV starts to roll a thick gray line dividing each frame my fist smashes the side of the box and it stops good thing to I was going to pull a gun and kill the fucker so you know exactly how the girl was canceled I ask the two officers the tall lanky one pulls the black cover back revealing a face met with blunt trauma the skin black purple with blood collecting around and in the various abrasions on her skull and body her arms badly scared and scabbed the officer replaces the cover letting it drop back over the victims head big time junk injector I signal for two men in white jump suits to take her away they slide her into the back of an ambulance box like red and orange leased to the county off to the morgue in a cushion of bluish fumes one machine for both the living and dead like a tree that grows in a forest only to be cut down and becomes a highly polished casket no one will see after its lowered in the ground out there lumber is growing for each of us waiting to be cut shaped and crafted into the final container and for what nothing makes any sense and no one cares when you're gone and there are no answers to anything except who did what and when and even those answers are not clear at times makes you think there's no point to any of it or if there is a point you can't find it or never will I walk away from the scene get into the car and drive towards the city the air not yet yellow and gray with black industrial smoke stacks that color the sky like bad crayons nothing on the radio except screaming preachers and right-wing mad men yelling about the end of time and how the whole world is going to the swish crowd I punch a hole in the window cracking the glass my wrist bleeding I stand watching the blood grabbing my wrist trying to force more blood out ready for an unmarked grave I take two steps back and fall on the bed the needle sticking straight out of my arm like a dart board in the next room I here the radio blasting race results I'm dizzy and headed for a blackout maybe this time I have reached the end a project I've been working on since birth trying to crawl back to the dust and shit I came out of my eyes focus on an envelope and a gun on the bedside table I start to lose my focus what a shitty way to go out in a small room in NYC I fight to stay with it got to know and feel every second his body stretched out on a small bed covered with dirty sheets he fixes his eyes upward not making a move not because he wants to because he has no choice he is paralyzed and believes he is dying his body cold to the touch inside he is warm very warm hot black moves across his vision like oil on still water he is out cold nothing apart from the sound of his labored breathing and city traffic outside people move live their lives inside he is out and the world moves on without him like a man standing on a dock watching a boat pull away on a foggy coastal morning nothing but the sounds of trucks chugging up the interstate I can't stand it anymore there's nothing in this fucking motel room and I can't go on I'm trapped as much as I try the bag of meth keeps calling the bottle sits and stares at me I turn the TV volume up the set vibrates with sound the cheap speaker straining against the onslaught of electrical energy trying to override the chemical's call there's someone next door the mother fuckers I hear them I swear one word out of them and I'll kill them I turn the volume down and jump up off the bed holding the bag in my hand I squeeze its contents the crystalline bits shift from side to side like bits of sugar hands shaking I drop the bag back in the drawer and throw myself on the bed holding my hands to my head everyone is talking and no one is listening the sound of voices shrill and aggravating scraping and grinding shrieking and screaming I know I'm fucking going to go mad right here and now in the middle of the desert I see myself on the wall in a white square walking the earth's crust over the brush and sand in the middle of nowhere to die alone I have to get a grip to stay alive I go to the bathroom splash cold water on my face look at myself in the mirror I notice my skin is dry and flaking but I'm not about to put any of that crap Ruth kept wanting to put on my face I walk down the halls green and white with scuffed brown base boarding and faded tiles no amount of buffing is going to help this floor too many felons and too many dicks have walked these floors in the sterile industrial law and order light back at my desk I start running through names of known felons with drug or sex connections the green and white lined computer paper in my hands containing people with lives and pasts how many had parents who beat them or fathers who never came home it's not my job to worry about these things yet every hour it gets harder to work these names this slime on a bed of green and white the clock says four in the morning I hear people and voices hard to keep my mind on things I think about the warmth of Ruth's arms and the smell of her all over me in my mouth and breath and I can never seem to get enough of her best I can figure out only twenty-five names on this list live anywhere near the crime scene I run a red pen laying out a bright ink trail around each name the impersonal type from the printer making it easy it's always easy when you look at people as numbers names or statistics maybe that's the problem I keep seeing faces and names and bodies and lives Christ I have been at this too long man this must be the longest fucking night in the history of the fucking human race I must look like a plant out in the sun too long hair matted from sweat clothes wrinkled and smelly I lean back my elbows on the bed there's one of those nine-hundred ads on the screen girl looks great good T & A on late night TV her name is Gloria and she says I should call her if I'm lonely fuck yeah I'm lonely wouldn't you be Gloria baby if you were in my loafers I pick up the phone dial the number I'll use one of my twenty stolen cards wait until some dumb ass gets the charge for this little call the line rings four times a female voice answers I want to talk to Gloria baby I hold the phone in my greasy fingers my eyes running up and down the dirty seam in the wall paper faded fucking flowers it's always faded fucking flowers in these places is it the flowers or is the wall plain brown I can't tell another little screw through the skull to remind me in a not so gentle way I'm loosing my coins I come to the gun still on the table next to the envelope for a split second I thought I was six years old again and in bed between fresh washed sheets the smell of life still good sweet instead a foul pile of rotten shit my eyes lock on to the envelop I don't want to open it and I don't want to know what is in it they'll keep calling until I do or kill me because I won't I'm in too deep now to back out they've got too much on me the fucking China White dangle and the thing with the Pope unless I do what they say I'm one dead mother fucker I hold my wrist up in front of my face the blood has scabbed making little islands they remind me of rust the kind you find under bridges and the undercarriages of cars the envelope is there the envelope must be opened the assignment taken the envelope the fucking envelope I want to run but there's nowhere to go and nowhere to hide I pick the envelope up and dangled it by the edge in front of my face hold a lighter under it and consider burning it and taking my chances the odds are slim and I carefully tear open the side a slip of yellow paper falls out and glides to the floor I reach and pick it up it's carefully folded in two the paper crisp to the touch I unfold the paper slowly inside there's half a newspaper clipping it falls out and there's a time 6:30 pm Tenth and Howard and the words I'm from Julius typed so impersonal so exact nothing more needs to be said I get up from my desk and head to the wants and warrants area and ask Haydee the woman behind the counter to have the names I've circled picked up and brought in she smiles and says sure Tom she's Cuban with corn yellow hair and a broad nose I often wonder if there is Indian blood in her and I remember before Ruth came along having bad fantasies about her those mahogany lightly oiled legs and pouting Spanish girl lips her red blouse set against her dark skin like hanging a sign out announcing I'd be a fiery lover and man I'll bet you she is I walk back to my desk and phone forensics anything on the finger prints yet drawing circles around and around on a pad of paper like a lost ice skater on hold waiting always on hold maybe I should have been a telephone sales consultant code word for boiler room smoke filled hard sales no money permission to give you shit for calling no thank you got enough troubles I read off some fuck's card number and a sexy sounding woman comes on the line hi this is Gloria let me make every dream of yours come true is this really you Gloria right off TV oh baby baby baby yes it's me and what's your name and what can I do for my man I stutter can't talk you can get me the fuck out of this shitty motel room is what you can do you can be my fucking link to reality you can be a real person so I know this life is real that's what you can do you can tell me if I cut myself I'll bleed and it will hurt that's what you can do because right now I'm dancing out here without a net you understand and I'm not sure what's real and what isn't and how many poor fucks are there across the country turning old and crazy under false manmade lights in shades of yellows and whites wondering the same fucking thing I stop to listen there's nothing there the line dead the whore hung up on me I slam down the phone pick the gun up I'm going to fucking use it this time the barrel scraping against loose scalp I drop to my knees he points the barrel to his temple and cocks the trigger the room is quiet nothing except the TV and distant sounds of tires hissing on the interstate he continues to hold the gun panicked not sure what to do it would be so easy he calls for his finger to squeeze the trigger nothing happens the message is sent there's no response his nerves and muscles dead he's held in check can't move or think how long he stays this way is unimportant for he has no knowledge of time passing it's him and the gun and the decision his hand shakes eyes shut tight in a very slow deliberate motion he lowers the gun and sets it down wipes his sweaty hands on his pants and goes back to the phone God damn will this night ever be over I'm going to fucking go mad I grab the phone call back gun in one hand no no I want Gloria I talked to her sounds from the TV rise and fall something about a miracle mop of some kind more shit for middle America oh yeah I won the lottery and I jammed every cent on the miracle mop and every other fucking item I saw on TV now I'm broke I don't know where it all went Gloria where the fuck is Gloria a female voice comes back on the line calm down honey I'm right here tell me what's bothering my exciting sexy man I know you're Gloria and you can't believe what's going on here I'm in this shitty motel room in the fucking middle of nowhere calm down baby and let Gloria get hot with you now what does my man want Gloria to do with him I finally get through to forensics Baby Doc Dan comes on the line yeah Daddy O we found threads and bits of fabric she definitely struggled before she was killed and there were grains of what we think is crystal meth strewn around the body and the apartment and dig this the killer left us a few calling cards blood his hers and a shoe print OK stay on it I mumble dead tired the line up should happen soon maybe we can cage us a squealer out of the group of twenty time losers the smell of fear runs wild over them it's enough to make you want to shoot every one of them outside the offices there's a sick banging and scuffling a hyped up crack head trying to shake off six badges they wrestle him to the ground reminds you of a kids pilling up at a high school football game only the wrong side keeps winning another white boy gone bad they get him cuffed and drag him screaming and yelling down the waxed hallway his ankles manacled by white plastic straps feet trailing the rest of his body the bottom of his dirty socks disappear around the corner I don't want you to do anything to me Gloria I want you to listen I'm on a fucking twisted power ride into insanity I got no booze just a bag of meth downers and some smokes and no past and no future do you hear me Gloria Gloria do you fucking hear me I hear you sweet sexy baby don't you want Gloria to help you let the stallion out of the corral to run you got to be kidding me you whore what kind of dumb gash are you sitting there repeating those bull shit phrases what you got them written down on a card is that how it works I mean if I call back as someone else you'll ask me the same fucking questions don't you get what I'm trying to say here

I'm walking the edge sweetheart I need a human voice to keep my feet on the ground to help me make sense out of this bull shit and you want me to get it up and jack off to your baby talk you got to be walking on the wrong side of the street here glamour puss I'm hanging out here on a thin thread and you act like you want to cut it off with a big fucking pair of scissors hello hello it's 6:30 nighttime I'm standing on the corner of Tenth and Howard the wind trying to bore through my clothes it's a cold night and the rain paints life in streaked in garish reds and blues there's maybe one other person on the street an old wino done up in burlap sacks he stands under a door arch holding a paper bag passing time waiting for God knows what even his skin looks better than mine good now if I could only crawl into it and give him mine but that's not going to happen so fuck it a skanky looking woman in her thirties gives me the once over with her burnt sad eyes and then walks up shows me a half a piece of paper and breaths I'm from Julius her breath is fowl face a mass of acne scars and bad teeth the two front ones discolored like Indian corn kernels you use to see in the Fall around Halloween I show her the other half of the paper and she shoves a fat dirty brown envelop in my hand instructions inside she says don't open it here how about if I open you up right here Sister I say she glares at me and says I don't move in your circle and what circle is that I ask Vogue People Magazine the Calle' Drug Cartel circles where there are balls and dicks something you'd know nothing about she yells and heads downstairs to the trains I stand there the smell of rapid transit and burnt oil drifting up from the shaft below in pools of black smudge this fucking city I walk to a chili parlor get inside and slowly rip open the brown well-handled envelope hello where the hell is that bitch Gloria I dial back wanting to yank the phone out of the wall and throw it around the room like one of those steroid geeks in the Olympics his body taut he yanks the phone out of the wall the line trailing behind like a dead snake he grabs the cord and starts to swing the phone over his head around and around and around and around and around and lets go the phone impacts the wall exploding in a shower of black plastic and plaster he sinks to his knees the broken instrument a tangle of wires and metal smiling back at him and he wants to smash it again instead he hauls it to him by its wire tail and examines the damage resigned to the fact he'll have no telecommunications for the rest of the hellish night instead he jury rigs the phone like a fighter who needs a cut man in the 6th a voice comes back on the line it's her look baby I gush I don't want to sit here in the middle of this shit hole stroking it to your hot talk I can get as much pussy as I need for real I just want a human voice to talk to can you dig their ready for the line up I walk down the hall my eyes like two camcorders making no value judgments just doing my job I take a seat next to two other homicide dicks Bronson and Hernandez Bronson is smoking his cigar the smoke gently bumping up against my nose if I shut my eyes I might be able to imagine this as a tobacco store filled with men in wrinkled tweeds smoking and talking no way to make that one go it's a line up and I watch the lights dim the suspects are paraded out to stand and face the glare of the yellowish spots each man appears uncomfortable and each looks guilty and each man tries to look tough their backs against the wall painted with black lettering and numbers a patrol officer escorts a woman in who has come forward to tell the police she thinks she might have seen the offender leaving the scene she remains standing a young dick with a baby face pulls the mike towards his unshaven chin making a metallic stretching sound the stem creaking his eyes read the instructions slowly there is a map and a date and time and instructions on where to score the junk and cash I know what they want and why they picked me because only a fucking junkie down and out loser asshole on the march would get into to this kind of a dead end deal I pick up a fork from the table and stare into its dull sheen and wonder what it would be like to wash one of these suckers day in and day out minding your own business instead of killing people to get by I examine the nicks and scars from the daily use the fork like my insides cut and tarnished the shine gone from over use I slip the fork in my pocket a symbol or a reminder of what I am and don't want to be I walk along the sidewalk looking at the cracked lines like tree roots or spider webs etched in dirt and dog shit cement and buildings bare and exposed things are breaking up by the second in this fucking city peopled down in the middle of the street either dead drunk or stoned beyond movement smashed crap scattered everywhere cars broken into and left to rot like broken molars it's enough to make you want to vomit we keep waiting for the end maybe the end has already come and we don't know it I walk into a triple decked mall done in chrome and steel kids running everywhere up and down the ramps and crowding the elevator maybe heaven is when your young and don't know any better or maybe only some kids go to heaven Daddy's charge card in hand the rest of us go to hell the second we're slapped on the ass crawling through life with the sting of the belt on your backside and the contemplation of violence in your heart the woman in her middle fifties is clearly nervous and I tell her there's nothing to be afraid of the suspects cannot see her she is dressed in green polyester pants and scuffed brown shoes that want to turn up at the ends her hair is bleached blonde and in the small space the sweet suffocating smell of perfume mixes quickly with cigar smoke OK stand straight and face the light the baby face detective barks into the microphone all but one obeys and a uniform cop turns him around the woman studies the men standing like frozen bowling pins she looks long and hard the dick makes them face left and then he makes them turn right after a few seconds she turns to the officers and shakes her head slowly it's a no go she couldn't tag one of them thank you ma'am another dark hole and no light I go to my desk and dial the phone the sound of her voice makes me hard I think about those legs and ass this woman soft and warm and a heart to match it makes my throat tight I listen to her yawn yup been up since early this morning middle of the night if you want to know the truth meet you for lunch in the same place you bet I'll even pay this time what you think about that baby I hang up and re-dial again look let me talk to Gloria look Gloria yes yes here's my credit card number yes Visa now what I want to fucking tell you is I don't want and need that fake jerk off sex and I don't care where you live and who you are I just want a fucking human voice to talk to why is it so hard to understand wait let me turn down the TV some movie on about a cop his pinch and a killer look I'm out here in the middle of fucking who knows where and I saw you on this ad on TV and you looked like someone I could talk to for Christ sakes I know you're no social worker or shrink but what the fuck do you care as long as the meters running and you don't have to talk dick sucking shit to some fat moron who's trying to get one up I need the sound of a human voice and I have to know there's someone out there besides me that is connected and gets it you dig there's silence on the other end I'm listening I ask her do you ever wonder why life is not like the movies why things never turn out the way their supposed to no matter how hard you try and do you ever wonder if God singles people out for cruel and unusual punishment and when he does it's like turning a gigantic screw and every day you live he turns it tighter and tighter until you cry and scream inside because the pain is so immense and then you cast a glance around you and see other people as happy as they can be and you can't figure out why that isn't you and what did you ever do to deserve the Lord's giant screw and why you had an old man who had to play fucking games with your head and twist your heart up when he was a grown fucking person and should have known better but either didn't or didn't give a shit and you had a mother who claims she never saw any of it and the only thing on your mind was killing the leading male member of the fucking household and you start to think the devil's inside your head and your heart and your fucked for life no matter what you try and so you resign yourself to the fact your ass is nothing your ass does not fucking count and you want it to be over with but it never ends do these things ever run through your mind coming at you like lighting speed and your head ends up like a mass of tangled strings where you can't free one fucking strand from another and nothing ever makes sense and let me throw this thought in also do you ever wonder why you can't be happy and that every fucking second you're looking for a new kick or jolt and the everyday pain of being alive is really the everyday pain of boredom's hold on and do you think sex can be the same as death the final act to either end or begin something I let the phone drop and get the bag of meth and quickly lay out two lines the sweet sweet powder the burn of an old friend and foe tearing up the inside of my nose and licking at the chemically stained meat of my brain we meet at the High Ace Motel in La Hambra and get the key walk hand in hand to the room her finger nails ruby red and her hair as dark as a raven's shiny feathers her green eyes make my stomach jump in the noon day light he sits and watches her slowly take off her clothes a sight he's witnessed many times never can get enough of it a thirst only her skin can quench his eyes move up and down her legs long movie star like the pictures of Rita Hayworth dance in his head pictures from movies they'd been to he feels like Bob Mitchum and no matter how hard he tries to figure it out he never can

understand what she is doing with him watching her undress
he tries to document every moment in his head naked they
tumble into bed and it becomes like one of those corny movies at the Egyptian she's hot for him and he feels the moisture
between her legs with little or no effort and he moves into her
lost in her smell and taste his smog tanned arms on her rusty
red skin the room a blur of colors and sounds he wonders
why they couldn't stay this way every day every hour every
second slow electric charged sex and gentle soul healing he
takes her from behind the both of them falling over when
their done not saying a word each lost in their own thoughts
she lights a smoke her long fingers fondle the tube of tobacco
everything she does is sex I don't need any sex I'm watching
two people on TV in bed right now he's kind of fucking ugly
she's a stone fox long black hair and legs up to the ass that's
not what I want to talk about Gloria don't you understand I'm
here in nowhere land lost cut off and I'm at the end of the
whole fucking thing and I have to make it until the morning I
know the morning is only a couple of hours away it seems
like it's been three am for ever oh God why can't you listen
I'm paying for it how hard can it be you fuck no no I didn't
mean you were a fuck he moves between her legs again he
rides her hips and she thrusts forward under him he feels like
he's going to pass out every ounce of blood in his system
pounding his head he never wanted to be this crazy about
anyone her reddish pink skin all over him strands of onyx
black hair in his mouth his stiff member moving in and out of
the shafts of daylight forcing themselves into the room they
roll over and back on the bed and she arches her back nipples
hard and ready I sit down and break down my thirty-odd-six
cleaning the oily skin and making sure the trigger will fire
with a squeeze yes the junkie as the skilled mechanic I'll only
get two shots off if I'm lucky so I have to make sure this thing
works anyway you examine the situation I'll be a dead man
after this anyway I screw and unscrew the various parts and
oil and check and oil and check rolling a tiny screw between
my thumb and forefinger there's something about killing I like
and if I get killed in a away I'll kind of welcome it and maybe
I'll get in the Times or the Post not bad for someone who
hasn't done much with their life except take other lives and
jam a needle in his arm I put the riffle part down and stare at
his picture black white gray smiling and waving to the crowd

I'll aim for the bridge of the nose and take him right out before a single person can guess what went down and make my escape and if I make it I'll be in Mexico by sun up the next day and he'll be dead dead for fucking up the family's business dead for fucking up the company's plan by taking the cash and never coming through with the vote his vote the key vote dead because they have me on the dangle and I'll have to do it my name and picture linked with his a senator and a junkie holding historic hands down through history there's a part of me that digs it we'll both go out being somebody and there's a part of me that wants out of the hell I'm in killing for junk and cash or being killed because I've become fucking baggage I put the photo down and sit on the bed pull my kit out of my sock and start to fix the smell of the match and the brown encrusted spoon fill the room he cooks it ever so slowly and filters it with a tiny cotton puff into the shiny reed thin shaft and draws it up the brown liquid waiting to integrate with his blood a long plume of red blood like a rocket trail works its way up the glass shaft he plunges the mixture in and tracks it creeping up his body heartbeat by heartbeat swathing him in a warm drowsy state escaping the pain of the ticking clock and the movement of the sun and the rotating of the earth on pain filled axis I leave her at her car and walk to mine she said nothing after we were through making love and I know what's in her head marriage and I want it some days and some days not something's holding me back I can't ask or agree the smell of her on me makes me lonesome the idea of kids and rings scares me I'll have to make a choice soon I pull up to the station parking lot among heavy Detroit iron in reds and blues back at my desk nothing on the case the wheel drags on I call down to the lab and they've got the victim's name and it's been sent to records which means sometime this afternoon I'll have to make the call to next of kin my eyes swollen and red the nerve endings floating on a sea of acid I hang up on the fucking cunt Gloria and peak out the window the sun's up now fucking A I made it through at least this part of the shit the madness still bouncing around the inside of my body like a whacked out pin ball that refuses to obey the laws of gravity bad shit is going to happen today I know it and God knows it the Devil's little child gone wrong in America going to give some pain I grab my stuff and hit the interstate moving deeper into the desert passing signs for truck stops and Indian jewelry good to be out of the fucking room maybe I'll call Gloria at the next fucking stop for what I don't know maybe it's to play with her head or play with mine and why can't she see what I'm trying to get at four walls in a motel room can kill you faster than four walls anywhere else I don't know what it is about her I'm drawn to her can't leave it alone it's like I'm arm wrestling with her and myself and the world my eyes park in the rearview mirror there's a cop behind me my heart jumps I clench the steering wheel knuckles white and tight to keep my drug driven fingers from shaking he's been on my tail for a mile he follows behind like a meandering calf following it's mother the thin steel whip antennas dipping back and forth cockroach like when I change lanes he changes lanes I know I'm going to have to kill this lousy cocksucker it's always the same fucking story they'll never leave you alone so I'll get off here before he makes his move I exit at the first off ramp he pulls right behind me hits the lights they snap red and blue red and blue red and blue I finger the hardware on the seat next to me bag of meth in the glove box good-bye mother fucker you'll be walking in hell in matter of a few heartbeats we slow down at the shoulder of the access road bits of gravel and loose tar crackle under our tires I move the gun to my left he gets out of the car and approaches holster unsnapped he turns out to be a she I hand her my driver's license will I please step out of the car terror from head to toe got to act quickly before she calls for backup I step out close the car door she leans in to look at the gun and he hits her hands together like a sledge hammer she crumples to the ground he picks her up and drags her by the hair to the back of the squad car handcuffs her and tosses her in the trunk pulls his car off the road and gets in the marked unit guns the engine and drives off swerving and fish tailing in the gravel off the road the car jumping and diving over cactus and rocks bumpy he comes to skidding halt and parks under a tall barrel cactus deep green scared long spines sticking out like the plant has undergone to many acupuncture sessions he rips her out of the trunk by her feet the sun is high and hot she's not bad looking he thinks dark haired pixie looking short shapely and well put together he stands over her scanning appetite wet hungry I reach for the phone to make the call it rings twice an old lady's voice says hello hello I say this is Detective Lou Bills of the Los Angeles Homicide Squad you have a daughter

Karen Ann Smalls silence on the other end a weak yes ma'am I'm sorry to have to tell you this she was found dead this morning around three AM you wouldn't have any idea who could of done this silence she was a good girl but we didn't know to much about her life I wanted to say they're all good girls you'll need to make arrangements to claim her body here's the number for the Coroner's Office read the number thanks good-bye click hands on forehead bad part of the job back to follow up motion over Jimmy Suarez check on any and all stolen vehicles in and around and after the time of the snuff let's see what we come up with if the mope took off maybe he ripped a rail job to make a getaway getting away from the scene will be tough I get up off the bed stagger a little throw cold water on my face got to cut down on the geezing for the job ahead I throw on some clothes the wool from my jacket rubs my skin the wrong way smells like wino vomit I walk in sewage live in garbage grab souls live behind stained walls should have been aborted before birth it's an overcast day bed sheets yellow tinged in sweat and misery I ought to go to the top of this joint and jump get it over with what would it be like the body falling nothing to stop it time running out does your entire life flash before you if it does I'll skip the rerun mop top innocence of childhood gone how old was I when I blew my first victim off the planet had to be sixteen got fifty bucks for it and some change a stupid old cabby long barrel twenty-two in the ribs bang the mother fucker was decked staggered from the car sick to my stomach Beverly Hills days and New York nights gone forever caught less than twenty-four hours later off to the hall did three year jolt in the California Youth Authority never hit the joint again after that one kept on killing developed an attraction to it loved the inner rage turned to art filling a dry bath tub with your own liquid shit pretending it's bubble bath by twenty five into the big leagues and a heavy junk habit like a credit card with a rotting seductive hook in the gut and legs it puts you under another's thumb you got to turn the cash and on and on now this is a fucking high hit profile job fucking press everywhere oh Christ I'm going to end up burning for this one we call him Toots because he loves bean burritos Toots throws a stack of paper on the desk all the wheels ripped in a twenty mile radius of the job I flip through the names and locations how the hell we going to look for all these cars then it hits me like a kick in the

nuts I mark only the cars a few blocks of the scene how far
can a guy get on foot not far I pick up the phone feed the
information to communications watch for these vehicles driver
should be considered armed and dangerous I pick up a paper
clip and press it between my fingers feeling good maybe we
got something here or maybe not maybe he owns the car he
drove off in would you use your own car on a job like this I
flip back to photos of the scene glossy black and white shades
of gray doesn't appear planned his eyes stopped on the death
face eyes vacant like something inside is now siphoned out
pain released he wonders does the soul fly like a black dove
after it's over we'll find out in the end the question is how
we'll find out some will peacefully some will suffer all will be
anonymous even the most famous of us he thinks humans are
so tough yet strip them naked and they're so vulnerable the
soft skin bruises and turns purple and yellow as if our skin
were like bruised fruit no clue how this car thing could go
either way can't tell if the sun is out or not lost track of time
after tonight I have two days before I have to go to the ap-
pointed place at sundown and wait supposed to hit the the
family values target in the glare of the bright lights or through
the car window doesn't make any difference got to lay him
cold nothing left but yesterday's headlines out on the street
people bump me jolt me right and left I don't fucking care my
head not in the game I amble to a movie theater go inside it
turns out to be a fuck house two naked figures on the screen
I sit down alone the place stinks like cum and stale popcorn
the two figures tangle licking and sucking coming from the
screen it's two woman one on her back legs open like a port
for a docking space ship the other woman's head works between her legs in a up and down motion he drags the female
cop behind the car and pulls off her shoes and pants exposing
her white skin panty lines and he tears open her blouse little
breasts white and pink tipped against the harsh sun light she
comes to and screams the sound rolling over the open desert
and tries to kick and struggle it's no use and her struggling
and fighting pleases him feeds him encourages his pathology
he tells her he's going to have her and then kill her right where
she lays so she might as well try and enjoy it his eyes fixed on
the color of her hair and he pulls down his pants a man naked
enters the room his cock swinging back and forth he gets in
between the two woman and starts fucking one in the ass

while the other one sucks and licks both of them he forces himself between his victims legs and tries to kiss her she wraps the cuffs around his neck with both wrists and tries yanking forward trying to choke him he frees himself stumbles back coughing and gasping for air and punches her in the face once and then again the sound of bone cracking mixed with heavy breathing she turns her head trying to avoid a third blow he mounts her pubic mound black against her pale thighs the smell of her blood dancing in the still air all three bodies are moving on the screen it doesn't make any difference my head is not into it I sit there looking at the film no reaction my dead feet stick to the cement floor moaning and growing coming from the screen one of the women has a mole on her ass and I watch it bounce up and down a black ball ridding a wave of larger life flesh he forces his way in tasting the blood on the downed officer's lips he moves back and forth against her in a slow ragged motion she becomes a struggling small animal fighting for life and dignity he pushes harder trying to see her legs and breasts reminding himself of where he is and what he's doing the sand attaching its self to both bodies no matter how hard he pushes he can't seem to come the narcotic in his body restricting the flow letting him go only so far and then no more he tries to fight it and now there's two wars going on her's to get free and his to get off he works harder she fights more he feels himself about to explode grabbing her gun he gets off two shots to her head blood on the front of the car the ground on his arms and shirt he gets up staggers and fires another shot her body jerks with the impact of the round the woman on the screen is chasing the guy's cock like it's a wild snake just when he gets her lips around the head the film stops and burns in the projector like a giant brown flower opening pedal by pedal in fast motion a giant burn spot like cancerous cell the screen is hot white until the film is patched the few people in the theater say nothing they sit glued to the screen out of boredom or shame I get up got to get out and get fresh air in the street sweat beading down my forehead in the car back to the crime scene this time I'll canvas the neighborhood myself see what I can come up with while the others check into the stolen car aspect the area packed with cheap pink and blue stucco apartments paint faded and palm trees brown and yellow attacked and left diseased by smog the fronds bend and wave doing a death dance in the poisoned air trash and spent beer cans dead in the gutters welcome to Southern California now go home I pull the car over and hit a broken Childs' toy breaking it further on the lawn I step over a large pile of dog shit ring the buzzer on the first apartment the door opens a fat woman in a purple tent like getup hair piled high teeth gray and rotting like aged marble she peeks out from behind the door what do you want I flash the badge ask if she saw anything no and the door slams I stand there for a second knock again what is it you want she shouts the smell of starch and sweat in the air calm down ma'am or maybe you'd like to take a ride I could put that together if you'd like arms heavy with fat dimpled at the elbows trash TV in the background I told you I don't know nothin' she pushes the door shut I jam my foot in and wedge the door open maybe you'd like for me to do a little checking on your AFDC or maybe you'd like it if I gave the folks at unemployment a little call about your check her features soften I'm telling you the truth officer I didn't see nothin' the first I knew about it was on the news like everybody else she always had men coming and going out of her place we all knew what she was doing but what business was it of ours I write in my notebook thank you for your time I step down the walkway to the next apartment abandoned spider webs hang in the corner of the buildings dead plants dot the mud filled planters I ring the next buzzer a little girl opens the door large brown eyes runny nose and dirty mouth flowered dress stained and dirty feet bare unwashed is your Mom at home no she answers hanging on the door knob a loud voice in the background who's at the door Lilly the little girl doesn't answer thin skeletal man with orange hair comes to the door gently pushes the little girl aside what's the story here what do you want I explain he says nothing claims he doesn't know anything and minds his own affairs and what are your affairs I ask his eyes narrow what does that mean don't play coy with me you know what I mean needle marks on his arms smell of booze on his breath oh shit I don't need this call for backup no choice maybe get something here more than likely another pain in the ass junkie case he scoops up her spent body red ants dot her head drinking from the dark skull wound ruby red he stuffs it in the trunk of the patrol car and hurries back to his own car he takes another snort of the meth the sand like grains snapping his head back he bellows at the top of his lungs his voice walking the barren landscape and hits the gas sand spraying everywhere gun bouncing on the seat next to his cars tires contact pavement with a screech I ease back let the speed stay at no more than sixty five the warm wind pouring in through the open windows I scream again and grit my teeth grinding molar against molar the smell of gas and oil like a ripe toxic fruit making me giddy like a crazy fly dipped in syrup I pass trucks and cars loaded with ordinary people if they only knew I could kill each and every one of them I am the fucking Pol Pot of the desert and to think soon I'll be in Mexico and be free I kill again and leave no trace for I am a fucking crazed genius a chemically tinged snake ready to strike blue sky and hot sun ride right along with me drive drive drive I climb out of the subway tunnel dank oil fume smell been wandering the streets the whole day examining and reexamining my problem like one of those small wooden cubes you try and pull apart I know I have to go check out the sight and case the place can't make myself go instead I duck into another coffee shop order it black watch the waitress' legs tight in flesh colored nylons makes me want to go home with her lay in bed her warmth keeping the shit and sadness out filling me up and flooding me with sunshine and sweetness no one dies we live happily ever after like there's a fucking tooth fairy and Christmas is great only to find out Santa's a child molester she pours me another cup and I thank her she smiles how do I make conversation how do you break out of your own self imposed isolation to try and touch another human a vow of silence and disassociation this has always happened with me cold sweat running down my forehead never knowing what to say like I've been dropped in a large room full of strangers with only my underwear on how many times have I had dream eyes frozen cold covered by silence and embarrassment oh god I'm loosing it you say you'd loose your mind if you tried to keep track with the amount of men who came and went out of her apartment well try and remember or I'm going to throw you in the can and the state's going to take the little girl and you can kiss this good-bye I gesture broadly with my free hand he lets me in the joke box joint done in Salvation Army rescue mission decor trash candy bar wrappers empty coke and beer cans children's toys soiled diapers a human refuge dump I'm going pop this white boy trash s.o.b. but first things first tell me what you know you say the last car you saw was a white Chevy did you get a plate number I

know you have better things to do and why would you spend
all day and night taking down plate numbers OK what year
was the car what do you mean you don't know don't screw
with me or I'll come down hard on you now what year was
the car was it a late or early model I watch his rotten teeth curl
around his thin junky lips for a dime I'd smash those dead
ivories right down his throat she moves to fill my coffee again
for the third time, and this time I take a gamble and gently
touch her hand our eyes lock she seems to read me like an
open file folder come back in an hour she whispers that's
when I get off I smile drop some money and walk out into the
cold letting the wind and gray sky punish my body sexual and
personal relationships are not a performance sport and you're
under no obligation to make this woman panic starts to work
it's way into every cell in my body the more I step the more I
get in it what are the chances of this happening to me or
anyone three cups of coffee and now I'm going to meet her
she sees in me what I see in her the two of us bolted down to
a life with no positive end both of us wanting to belong to
someone anyone last room on the right fine the Thermal Motel rooms by the day or week me and maybe three other fucking
people I check in hit the air close the drapes horses and cow-
boys jumping across the pleats in the bedspread I lay out a
couple of lines and turn on the burn the rush hits hard I jump
to my feet and start dancing around the room wired out of my
cranium the buzz zipping and zapping through my body haven't
slept in three days going mad like a rat too long in the heat
can't get my mind off Gloria turn the radio on cheap plastic
simulated wood grain country music hate that shit there's so
much shit in the air can't fucking hear anything settle on a
Mexican music station mas musica y todo mundo blah blah
blah crack the seal on another fresh bought bottle the drink
chasing the powder the thought blows across my brain maybe
later I'll go kill the cock sucking desk clerk cash low the fucker
will go over easy also got to have another set of wheels maybe
take his car nothing happens until dark got to talk to my baby
Gloria and then I'll put the asshole to sleep one less fucking
mouth to suck air off the planet no point in this guy living to
see tomorrow good night mother fucker I lay down on the
bed wallpaper a ruined brown color yellow water stains in the
upper corner another shit hole I'm up again clothes off I step
into the hot water shower feels good whole body like charged

up amps running through it I get hard thought of the little
police girl the bitch was tight until the end I stroke my cock
the thought of her milk white thighs taste of her blood the two
bodies struggle in the sand her blood on his hands the taste
driving him on he paws and rips at her his head throbbing
pleasure mixed with anger so you don't remember the plate
numbers did you see anyone come or go beeper goes off you
got a phone I step over beer cans and old milk cartons dial in
Childs Juarez on the line highway patrol woman killed off the
Old 66 OK I'll wrap it up here and we'll head out to have a
look two dead in twenty-four hours this boy is heating it up I
walk out the front door in the car on the radio six two nine
Boy I call to have Child Welfare and the narc boys pick the
neck up and take care of the kid I throw it in gear and head
off to meet Childs it will take three hours to get out there I
wait in the corner she comes out white uniform hair pulled
back bundled in a heavy coat it's cold in NYC this time of year
we walk to a cafeteria two coffees sit at a table why did you
decide to join me it's dangerous to deal with strangers in this
city I ask her there was something about you maybe a lost
look I don't know why have I made a mistake I laugh and it
feels good no I don't think so I'm no priest if that's what you
mean I say nothing else no nobody is what they do for a living
what do you do for a living she asks what makes you think I
have a job you're in rather nice clothes and that's a nice watch
you have on and you said about living and jobs plus I see a lot
of people in my line of work she laughs we sip coffee I'm in it
again not that I've had that many women in my life but now I
have someone I would have to explain things to it's the last
thing I need yet she seems so lost like me trapped no way out
I'm drawn to her delicate child features and rough kitchen
hands a pull I don't need nor want can't move away from and
she's put herself in a position where she's locked onto me
God knows why do you not want me here no what makes you
say that smile on my face like a frozen shell you seem lost in
thought again the far away look I saw in the coffee shop let's
get out of here where do you want to go maybe just walk and
walk until we can't walk anymore I'll try but I've been on my
feet all day I sit on the motel room bed take another pull from
the bottle and turn on the TV a talk show of some kind people
talking about love with animals for God's sake you talk about
fucked up at least I like pussy in fact you could say some

43

women are dying to fuck me I roll back on the bed laughing man I'm going around the fucking corner going to try and lay off the dust tonight and see if I can get sleep the bedspread smells of stale smoke there's a shity looking picture of a bowl of fruit on the wall looks like it's made out of cardboard I try to take it off the surface to look at it further it's nailed down who the fuck would steal this crap I give a pull and it comes out leaving flakes of plaster on my hands and on the edge of the bed I get a knife from the pocket of my pants and pry the frame apart it is a piece of fucking cardboard nothing on the back but dead gray surface I sail it across the room in an arc it hits the drapes and settles to the floor below the air conditioner on the TV their showing a picture of some fat slob broad and her German shepherd she's talking about having sex with it I can't even feature it a dog wanting that piece of gristle we walked for a couple of miles and ended up at her place warm and small I ask to use the bathroom pink fuzzy rug on the floor with a matching one covering the toilet seat bottles of nail polish in the medicine cabinet ice tea colored bottles with child proof white caps laden with pills clustered in one corner on the lower shelf I go through them looks like some downers I dry pop a few and sit down to fix he holds a group of lit matches under a dirty bent spoon the powder bubbles into a brown liquid he loads drawing the nourishment into the syringe the tip of the needle bites and pushes through a clear patch of skin his blood mixing with the brown fluid like a small red tornado he forces the toxic syrup into his arm enough to stay well his body relaxes with the rush of the narcotic warmth done he flushes the matches and used toilet paper down the toilet rolls his sleeve down opens the bathroom door it took us three and a half hours to get to the scene the whole time all I could think of was Ruth it was a mess her body stuffed in the trunk of the car the smell was overwhelming her face a mess two bullet holes dark and encrusted in the head eyes vacant like she had fled her body for another place and left it behind to decompose black pubic hairs matted and stiff zip her into a black body bag the lab men work the sight for clues prints over here tire tracks the lab men get to work swarming the scene the state men in on it soon the fight will start as to who has first dibs on the asshole that did this us or them what's this guy's thing with women or did this one pull over the wrong kind of guy contents of the squad car emptied they

pick it up to take it to the state garage for a further exam
pictures taken right and left press boys right on the spot OK
let them in someone says another underpaid public servant's
life gone so some old jerk can write the newspapers about
rising crime and taxes you're a junky aren't you she asks I sit
down on her Sears and Roebuck couch the material knotty
reminds me of cream corn why do you ask I whisper the smell
of burnt matches and the look in your eyes do you often go to
a stranger's house and fix on the first date only when the
bands of pain tighten to the point I have to I say and half
smile did you want me to get sick right here I ask her my head
becoming heavy no I guess not go ahead and drop off I'm use
to it how do you know so much about it I ask my old man had
a sieve for an arm put everything we ever had into it rent and
food so I left home at 17 if you could call it a home to get
away from it and now here you sit maybe I ought to throw
you out oh don't do it not now I lean my head back I try and
sit by the pool but it's no good I'm to jacked to sit still my
knee keeps bouncing the fucker must have a life of it's own I
take a hefty swig from the bottle and walk back to my room
the news is on the TV I turn it up their talking about the
officer what kind of a sick man would rape and kill a little girl
like that her face pops on the screen dark hair high cheek-
bones a smile on her muzzle decked out in her uniform sudden
sorrow sweeps over me I feel sick I take both hands and make
an ax handle swing hard into the side of the TV it teeters and
falls off the stand in a crash of exploding glass and smoke I
stomp it over and over again with my foot the outer shell
bending and giving way to repeated blows crystallized glass
bits dancing on the carpet I drive my foot into the battered
body I drop to my knees pick up a sharp jagged slice of picture tube glass and run it across my wrist blood flowing from
under the skin sticky wet I don't want to live there's no fucking
point let them find my body bloated and stinking never yield-
ing a clue to what I've done blood on the carpet I feel sick
dizzy tired my head goes light the room goes black on the ride
back traffic is bad road construction everywhere marked by
yellow and red cones like rows of Halloween candies the radio crackles rolling out info on the latest labor strike somewhere
in Ohio and rain in the forecast Juan tells me to pull in at the
next Taco stand we see he's hungry man how can you be
hungry after what we've seen what does what we've seen have

to do with food and life you still have to eat don't you my
head might as well have been a filament in an old tube that
starts out weak and gets brighter as it warms up I open my
eyes and she and I are sitting in the dark a surge of panic runs
through me where am I and what day is it it's the same day as
when you came in here with me only it's night why do you
have to be somewhere nice company you come to my house
and then shoot your drugs crash out and now you want to
leave I thought may be I'd make us something to eat how long
has it been since you had something other than coffee and
doughnuts it had been awhile so I sat back on the couch and
watched her get busy in the kitchen she was light and delicate
looking yet tall at the same time with large eyes and a cute
face I didn't need any of it and I turned on the TV to drown
out the thoughts of her I saw him the senator giving a speech
his blow dry hair well kept maybe it wouldn't be so hard to
kill him after all he was dressed in a blue suit and red tie the
seal of the state of New York in front of him he was motioning
with closed fists blue curtains behind him I imagined them
stained with his blood the head snapping back violently from
the impact there would be those who outwardly would mourn
him yet secretly would be glad he was gone when I focused
again he was gone and they were covering a murder of a
highway patrol woman in California some fuck senator saying
maybe women weren't fit for field jobs in law enforcement
most in law enforcement weren't fit and even if they were
who'd want to take dump truck loads of shit from a dumb ass
public if it were up to me I'd kill every last person who gave
me any bullshit at all some cop I'd make I smell food coming
from her tiny kitchen white wooden cabinets and bluish walls
I don't know how to tell her I can't eat my life will come to an
end in the next forty- eight hours and if she's having a clean
up fantasy about me she better drop it right because I'm not
her father now Juan stuffs himself with burritos and coffee I
sip on a cola trying to sort out what I've learned in the last
twenty-four hours one stolen car two murders and the sweet
smell of Ruth thoughts of matrimony bounce in and out of my
head pulling me apart the last thing I want to do is get married
even though the taste is so sweet and once you've had it you
want more the want of it shredding your insides no way to kill
the sensation Childs asks me where I am wouldn't you like to
know I smile back we get in the car hit the interstate she

serves me a full plate of food on blue and green dishes with ruby red tumbler full of soft drink a tidal wave of nausea sweeps over me cold sweats coming on I can't eat and slowly push the plate away hand trembling not looking at her hurt face I stare at the table cloth its black color inviting want to tumble back to the days when it was kicks and chicks and there was no life or death no crank only the pungent smell from reefer on a Saturday night in the City Of Angeles I was hot then had people in my life and the touch of another mattered warm hands on me work their way up my cheek I ignore Childs and start to think about Ruth again I see her she's examining me why does she even care about someone like me what have I got to offer her the same thing my father offered my mother no clothes on I see us roll naked on my bed Ruth's fine slender body pink almost a red tint spread out before me doing battle with commuter traffic vying for my attention oh God I can't get enough of her I want to plunge in and suck her insides out touch and taste every bit of her flesh we roll over and over laughing I come to my head pounding glass sparkles like bits of rare rocks my mouth is sour with bile and blood on the carpet on my shirt my wrists scabbed and dried blood like used earth I'm a fucking mess if anyone had pounded on the door on account of the noise I wouldn't have noticed like to pull out a butcher knife and slice my brain in quarters like cauliflower then throw it away the sun orange and fighting the motion of the earth darkness oncoming got to get cleaned up have an appointment with the mother fucker at the front desk and I'll call Gloria if I can control myself for five fucking seconds I might beat this whole deal and get to meet this cunt Ruth lays in my arms her skin is so soft and smooth untouched and pure makes my head spin I always dreamed of a girl like this she looks like she jumped out of a milk ad hey baby are you hungry we dress and watching her put her clothes on he wants to take them off again slowly handling each bit of material her standing before him flesh exposed and trembling he feels every inch of her skin every bump every curve nothing else is alive in the world except her she's what counts nothing else no one else when he's hungry it's her when he's thirsty it's her she's like a trap a maze he can't get out of I'm brought back to the here and now by the honking of horns and bumper to bumper traffic behind we pull into the station I park the car and wonder if Childs can see the hard on in my pants I

step out of the shower pull on some clothes the first clean
ones I've had on in the two days since I've been on this crawl
I pick up the phone dial the number her voice comes on digi-
tally reproduced for my consumption Gloria it's me what do
you mean what can you do for me I told you I don't need any
fake pussy I want to talk hear another human voice I know
you know how fucking crazy life is and how painful it is trying to stay alive forced into doing things you don't want to do
people always talking bull shit and do you know Gloria there
are some people who have no right to live why are they here
and what do they do except breed like rats and rip you off
every fucking chance they get these are the ones you have to
do something about are you listening Gloria hold on a second
I'll be right back her hands are soft on my cheek she leans
over and kisses me I look at her my eyes ask why even though
I know why it has to do with the bullshit about her old man
because I feel safe with you she whispers and takes me by the
hand and leads me to her bedroom I lie down on the bed she
pulls off my shoes and then stands before me slowly removing
her clothing she sits next to me naked and kisses me again her
tiny breasts and sharp nipples should move me but I can't I'm
paralyzed by fear and junk an she gives up knowing it doesn't
do any good and she whispers it's OK after you've slept and
I've taken care of you we'll try again and I fight back the
feeling of being trapped and having to share the ugly truth
concerning my life with another with her and if she knew
what would she say and would those young pointed nipples
be so available to the fingers of a junky and a killer one who
does it for money one who does because he likes it the lines
of crystal meth are on the table and they burn my nose and
make my balls shrivel with hype and adrenaline so Gloria are
you there good where was I oh yeah so there are some people
who live and take from life and shouldn't be here with the rest
of us because they don't deserve to live and their asking to be
let go and they should be because they stink like a homeless
person who eats out of garbage or a woman who rips you off
using her pussy to get it done tell me why these mother fuckers
should be allowed to live she pauses on the other end of the
phone and my mind jumps like a grasshopper to the shit bird
at the front desk he only has a few more hours to live and
then I'm going to kill him and grab the cash it's not that I want
to I have to because I'm running out of money and no money

no shelter and no drink and no drugs and why should I let
him live no one will miss him and what great things has he
done to add to the pile of shit we're hip deep in so do you see
what I'm trying to say Gloria two murders tire tracks and a
stolen car isn't it enough to go on are you telling me no one
has seen that car in the last forty-eight hours I ask Childs and
the rest of the dick squad gathered around smoking and trying
to put things together yes we alerted the highway patrols in a
three state area Childs shoots back but where's that car now
how about a witness to the second murder Benson asks no
witness funny how no one sees anything when something goes
down unless it's a hand waver about a parker in front of a fire
hydrant the room bursts into laughter I get up to score a cup
of coffee knowing there's nothing to do but wait and hope for
someone to spot the car or find it abandoned on a side street
somewhere then it hits me it might be a blind lead but worth
a try I call Childs' name follow me lets search the place of last
resort I whisper no Childs moans not LAX you bet the airport
what else we got maybe he left the car there or she left it there
now you know no woman did this their not strong enough
speak for the women you know pal I shoot back we both
laugh I roll on my side legs feel like their being clawed and
each nerve and muscle pulled tight like suspension bridge
cables in a high wind I need a fix roll off the bed crawl to my
shoes pull out the works she's gone hands trembling I cook
and fix in the bedroom the pain slows and eases up I have to
get the installment of drugs and cash for the at hand I shower
leave no note and hit the street cloudy day sun out then gone
trees nothing but brown sticks and branches dead to the cold
on the subway I watch a couple of old people hugging each
other sadness seems to drip from every source a bucket of bad
hours and moments turned on its side insecurity spilled out its
black contents on my feet legs hands face oh to be old and
have it almost over or at least a reason for ending it trapped
halfway between young and old can't go back don't want to
go forward words out there mean nothing I meet my contact
on the subway platform the old box top torn in half trip given
a key to a locker inside the Port Authority building I go upstairs and board a bus to take a little ride try and throw off any
tails that might be hooked always a hassle for bread and junk
something not right here let me ask you this Gloria have you
ever thought about killing anyone silence a small voice no

what would you say if I told you I not only have thought
about it I've done it as well Gloria Gloria the phone dead
nothing the sounds of relays clicking I smash the phone into
its cradle lay out a couple of lines it burns before ignition grab
my gun every nerve in his body on bright red high alert tuned
in turned on ready to kill thoughts of the little police woman
race through his head like the clicking of a clock white thighs
black pubic triangle blood smell of his own semen he walks
through the office door the tiny man behind the desk looks at
him with his two small brown eyes he fires two shots splitting
the man's head in two his eyes roll back he slumps down
against the switch board in the background the radio plays as
if talking to no one he throws the desk clerk's body behind
the counter scoops the cash out of the drawer and walks out
as if nothing happened in the motel room I throw my shit
together going to gamble big on this pick the phone up dial
out I'm one crazy lemon sitting here daring them to come get
me take me now you mother fuckers nothing at the airport no
abandoned cars nothing so what now I ask Childs sooner or
later this guy will screw up and show himself we have to hang
tough we start back to the office lab working overtime on the
tire track Feds now in on the picture things have more than
gone to shit it's bad enough when the state boys get in but
when the Feds show up now the shit is really going to get
deep too deep for this citizen one of the three of us has to
come up with it or the newspapers start then the talk shows
and then we'll get shit from Justice and let's not forget the
fucking mayor and his crap just what we don't need or want
people are so vulnerable and they don't even realize it my
mind wanders cars everywhere stuck in traffic stop go stop go
turn the radio on nothing worth a shit no ball games today
mind wanders to Ruth's bare legs oh Christ got to get off the
subject or I'll pop one right here in front of Childs we ride in
the car say little blue brown haze hangs over the city and the
trees appear like their choking from the air hit the brakes Childs
screams a black BMW tinted windows tries to clear the inter-
section we collide with a bang thrown forward and snapped
back we're out of the car in the street the car must be hot the
passengers bail and start to run we pursue I'm on the radio
breath short Childs is out in front a crack rips through the air
Childs tumbles a gush of red is pouring out of his back oh shit
I keep going man down man down I yell into the radio back

inside the Port Authority there's a long row of beat up gray
and green lockers some with keys stuck in them some not I
move slowly make sure this is not a set up job trust no one I
knew a guy who once laughed at me for saying move slowly
check it out bet he's not giggling now unless it's with the devil
took the Feds three days to find the body parts I take a seat
across from the lockers and watch for awhile to see who comes
and goes first installment before I'm supposed to do the job
no hurry now hang back let the eyes search do what you
know is right people come and go they'd be fucking floored if
I could take what's inside my head and transfer it to the people
in this building they'd freak and run screaming into traffic
human shit splattered everywhere the things people do when
panic sets in the thought is there like creeping moisture on the
corner of a ceiling and starting to spread the thought laps at
me like an orange flame singeing the hair on my legs and
blistering the heels of my feet take the cash and drugs and run
run so far they'd never find me out on the beach under the
sun laying back shooting the whole ball of goodies up my
arms at once until it's over eat the dirt of Mexico or Chile gun
ready he goes down the alley slow light on his feet in the cat
prowl mode the narrow passageway ends in a T shape he calls
for cars on both ends these fucks could be anywhere waiting
he is shaken by his partner's death he pauses and takes a
couple of deep breaths tries to figure things out he starts down
the alley gun in hand there's no backup yet he moves anyway
trash cans appear almost like props in a movie set this can't
really be happening he thinks a flash of green is there and
gone he holds his gun out steady the radio crackles the dogs
are coming in he acknowledges with a ten ninety-nine and
holds his position the K-nine corps arrives and they ready the
dogs he moves back out of the alley the blue suits on their
way now do I sit it out here and act like nothing has happened no way this fucking car is hot I walk to it very slowly
get in and pull out behind the motel I think it's time I ditched
this bone yard survivor maybe I should take a bus would they
look there hell no ditch the car five blocks from the bus station and start walking the whole downtown if you can call it
that shut up tight looks like fucking main street USA wonder
what it would be like to grow up in this fucking place side-
walks small old store fronts man you dance with a cunt in this
town and you marry her bus station old off white building

brown wooden benches one window for tickets no activity couple of candy machines no bus until early in the fucking morning now what the fuck am I going to do out in the open feel like a snail pulled out of its shell fear starting to set in have to control it keep it down I get up walk to the small rest room it stinks of urine and shit throw cold water on my face get a grip survive endure it's the key the only key take a bus out of here to El Paso and jump across the boarder swim the fucking Rio Grande if I have to the silence is broken the order comes across the radio he moves out of the alley and waits at the opening the dogs are let loose barking and screaming one of the dogs has the driver of the car by the leg and is working its way up towards the crotch biting along the inside of the leg he runs down the alley blue flashes from everywhere guns drawn two suspects on the ground there's a third one out there they decide to split up he starts to search through the numerous backyards brain and nervous system on auto pilot eyes make contact he sees a flash of green and fires misses a slug whistles by he ducks fires again hits the green jacket once in the chest he goes down blood sputtering and foaming he calls for help dogs cops ambulance scream up the street third man fights to breath long blonde hair wet with sweat they take him off he stands not knowing what to say he did the right thing some how it doesn't seem right reminds him of when he was a boy had to fight he could and did win never felt right about it he remembers asking his old man about it and his father laughed and ran a rough hand over his hair time to make a move the lockers test safe and there appears to be no one in sight the key goes in and the door pops open wobbling a tinny thin metal tune inside a brown bag I stuff it in my jacket pocket and head out the door I'll take a cab this time no public transportation jump into a Yellow meter running right away bag safe inside my coat it would be so perfect except for the thing that has to be done the thing hanging over my head the thing I can't ditch no matter what someone must die someone must pay nothing for free dumb ass statements they mean zero not shit time crawls in this fucking place I've really fucked up now anger anger anger I want to smash something anything and if the little dickhead in the ticket window doesn't stop looking at me I'm going to feed him to the first black hole I can find want to scream God damn it want to gnaw someone's veins out of their arm shit can't take this anymore I get up take

a walk outside it's cold few nearby houses have gentle glows
of yellow and green coming from their windows bet they'd
shit if I broke in and killed them never live by bus stations and
graveyards is my motto I start across the street this is a bad
idea I know some bad shit is going to go down it floats in the
back of my head I'm powerless to stop it locked down on this
course in life and it doesn't matter what I want or what anyone else wants I keep moving towards death destruction and
sex want to drop to my knees and ask God to take me now
never get an answer so I keep walking there's a small wooden
shotgun style house on the end of the block I stand across the
street and peer in a young girl in white shorts and bare feet is
walking around holding a baby I pull back off the street into
the bushes stash my duffel bag pull out a little powder take a
toot like yanking the string off a top my eyes glowing in the
dark back in her apartment I open the paper sack stack the
money on the table pull out three small plastic bags of brown
powdered sweet medicine for the sick at heart pull open a bag
dip a finger in taste yes yes few things make me really happy
I stash it back in the bag push it under the couch I make a
note to swing by and pick up my equipment stored in a locker
at Grand Central have to come up with a way to get unhooked
from this woman hear her key in the door those legs and ass
so fine she has a brown paper bag in her hands she bends
down and gives me a peck on the cheek what the fuck is
going on here what am I doing this urge to tell her everything
works at me like my gut is a pressurized tank the gas of guilt
and truth pushing on the metal sides trying to escape I want to
I can't what the fuck am I doing what would she say if I told
her I'll be dead by the end of the week creeping along the
front lawn into a clump of bushes standing guard over the
house he looks in the window at the young flesh only her and
a baby he starts to get hard he thinks about her struggling and
it drives his body reckless with desire once you've killed it
gets easier that's what most people don't understand he tells
himself if he takes what's before him he'll have to kill her no
choice gun drawn I shoot he goes down it keeps playing in
my head over and over and over sit at dinner can't eat yes I
know honey I tell Ruth it was either him or me it doesn't make
it any easier you know Babe I can't tell you anything what
would you think if I told you there was also a part of me that
got off on shooting the guy maybe it was because I saw Childs

take one it's like these two fists inside my head hitting wanting to strike out no one values life anymore no one gives a shit and I'm so sick of the cliche's and political bullshit maybe I'm getting too caught up in it she smiles and looks at me my heart pounds aren't you supposed to get tired of a job or a person after awhile you've been through a tough time it will pass isn't that what you would tell me don't try to read too much into it she moves in front of the window white shorts dirty blonde hair pinned up behind her head she's small he eyes her like a monster chops wet smell of blood in the air he fights with himself he wants her but if he gets caught it's over is it worth it is anything worth it he walks around to the front door and knocks she comes to the door baby cradled in one arm is the man of the house at home he asks her legs look smooth and young no when do think he'll be back he's at work she answers swinging the baby back and forth I see OK thanks before she can shut the door he punches her in the face his body making one smooth motion starting at the shoulder and following through to the fist she tumbles backwards the baby hits the floor starts to scream he gently picks it up off the floor placing it on the couch she tries to run he tackles her forcing his hand over her mouth alone without Ruth I pour a shot and try and sort out what's gone on an unsolved set of murders and now a man who I worked with for ten years dead a car accident a funeral to go to the palm trees appear bent their fronds brown-tinged dying they must be tired of the sun tired of the smog tired of the whole fucking city I take another drink turn the radio on it's KABC and some woman is talking yelling niggers and crime sick bitch they think it's so easy I twist the dial to music it will be one of those rare nights when I'll have to drink myself to sleep something I saw my Dad do a lot of after the trouble down in South Central after sixty- five he was a good cop and cared so damn much it broke his heart I'm trying to be one too without getting my guts chewed up by the system I turn off the radio and turn on the television a man and woman are fighting on the screen he's dragging her into a bedroom she keeps trying to bite his hand and he hits her again throwing her down on the bed and grabbing some belts out of her old man's closet he ties her ankles and wrists down she jerks and pulls trying to get free he ties a part of a bed sheet around her mouth and pulls off the white shorts her little pubic mound glistens in the yellow light of the room he goes down and starts to work he finds no evidence she likes it the taste of her only excites him more her head jerking right then left trying to free herself the belts and sheet to tight and he knows he's going to fuck her and kill her for once I ate the dinner she cooked for me and it made her happy we sat drinking wine and she asked me where I had been today how was I going to tell her where I had been and what I had done so I told her I went out to look for work I lied deciding not to tell her a thing lies are better than the truth at times she asks me how I feel and I tell her fine the haunting paranoia and impending death job seems strangely unimportant grabbing my hand she leads me to the bedroom to try again for something I may not be able to give her there's nothing on TV and you'd think with the channels to choose from something would be there I take another drink and the phone rings and I make no effort to get up and answer it and the answering machine comes on and I hear her voice and I want to let her in I can't and wish my Dad was alive he would understand there are times when this job is so sweet and you feel so proud because you're doing something not just talking really doing something for someone else and then when it's bad and when you feel as if the only thing your doing is swimming through human waste with unsolved murders and the death of a friend you wonder if you're really doing anything or jerking yourself off with your gun and badge that doesn't mean shit to most people and even if you could kill every low life pig that walks the streets it still wouldn't stop the tide of pricks and rip off artists fucking over the weak and wounded on a daily basis she stops talking the answering machine clicks off her voice is gone I get dressed and aim the car in a familiar direction she's naked in front of me legs spread and I can't get it up and she takes me in her mouth and my body reacts never mind the drugs and end of my life right around the next corner my body reacts and I'm in her and we move and I think I'm going to loose it and I keep trying sweat clinging to my buttocks I force myself to stay in and stay hard until I can't hold it anymore and even though it didn't last very long for her she says it was OK with a smile on her face and I lay my head down on her chest she strokes my hair and I ask her why me and she asks me why does it matter and I doze off secure for the first time ever with another human being the level of light was low and it took me a couple of second to adjust to it walking among

the graves to where Dad is I sit down on the wet grass and
stare at the headstone what would you make of these murders
and Childs' death Pops I ask half out loud what has it become
and what does it mean getting inside her is a struggle and she
fights him and he pushes and she's tight and warm and the
baby is crying and he's pushing and she's trying to cry out and
a hand grabs his back and neck and yanks him off a tall husky
man is yelling in horror and rage and comes for him and the
two men wrestle one with his pants around his ankles he gropes
for the hardware gets one shot off slides out from under the
dead man a large red and black hole in the side of the dead
man's head powder burns charring the pink bruised skin power
burns on his fingers he gets up and kicks the dead man a
couple of times for good measure she lies still on the bed he
searches the kitchen finds a butcher knife runs it with careful
effort up her taught stomach parting the flesh as he goes guts
her from head to toe blood spills over the sides of the bed like
she were a large mammal being lifted out of the sea her blood
pouring out like water the blade makes for dull labor against
her skin when he finishes he drops the knife washes his hands
in the kitchen and walks out the back making his way to the
bus station to try and lay low until his bus comes the waiting
makes him nervous so he walks out to the highway and starts
to walk thumb out wishing for a car to come and give him a
ride a guy in a truck stops he climbs up and the truck lumbers
off like a giant steel and fiberglass green elephant a cop car
passes them from the opposite direction as they head towards
San Diego things are looking good again and he thinks of
Gloria and getting right figuring he'll lay out a couple of lines
in the john the next time they stop and maybe he'll call Gloria
where have you been I've been trying to call you all night we
got another one he struck again this time a young girl and her
father it's a mess I pause for a second let me take a shower
and I'll be right there I wake with a start my head still on her
chest she kisses me deep hard I try to give her all I have we
work on each other with hunger and skill I'm half in half out
where am I going and what am I doing I give into it a swirl of
soft skin and smells sex is a fucking drug no shit if he's going
to commit a murder why do it out in some God damn place
like Victorville shit I don't say anything I don't like this guy
Arthur Stickboys no one does so this guy has to drive way out
here and have himself a little fuck party shit by the time we

get there it'll be morning another killing another body what's the point I say nothing watching the cars go by in the night withdrawn inside myself throat idle nothing to say my head numb still I let Artie do the talking this is a joke the guy's in Mexico by now you can bet on it so what do we have now three four murders that we know of who's counting the families we pull into a small truck stop I hit the john lock the stall it smells like shit in here lay lines out on a matchbook burns the nose and throat makes you experience something between God and fucking Hitler jumpy jumpy out in the fresh air the meth drips down my throat I chase it with an orange drink munch on a candy bar we're back in the truck again he talks about his life wife kids a square john type everything that would make me feel like a prisoner and then I wonder why I never went down that road and long for one place one woman and then I think about my fucking parents and I don't want to ever see anything like that again I should kill my stepfather now that I'm piling a few bodies up you know the thing that's got me why no roadblocks maybe they think these killings are the work of a couple of people I'm a fucking pro got to have wheels I think I'll loose this blue collar jerk off at the next town and snatch some iron I want to eat some road snort my way right to the Mexican boarder enough of this wandering around in the desert waiting to die fuck it the murder scene is a mess blood splashed everywhere the girl's body suspended by belts over the bed like a hunk of beef blood once red with life now black in death hounded by a halo of black flies I had to step outside and get some fresh air call placed to the Feds bring them in to help set up a meeting between them the locals here and our troops see what we have and see what we can come up with case the area foot work ask those near by why didn't anyone hear anything got any clues Art for once is quiet we're all quiet nothing to say it has to be one person state orders roadblocks on the major highways nothing we can do about side roads for another couple of hours until the sun is up higher then we'll get a chopper I call Ruth get her out of bed yeah baby it's bad real bad could be the same guy don't know when I'll be home when I can love you baby we lay in bed the TV on the question comes like I knew it would what do you do for a living Bobby there is a quiet in the room only the noise from the TV surges up to cover the black silence I told you I'm a consultant a consultant she asks what kind of consultant has your kind of a drug habit look what ever you do it's OK with me don't you think I have a right to know it's not that you don't have a right to know it's that you'd be better off not knowing her eyes tell me she doesn't buy it I roll out of bed reach inside my shoe and pull out my works go to the bathroom close the door going in there and hiding from me with your drugs and this door isn't going to answer my question she yells the door moves under the force of her banging on it I knew it would come to this and I should have walked away or smoked her look I tell her listen to me you don't want to know it's better if you don't ask it doesn't work and she pounds on the door even louder he gears the truck down and that's a good thing because I'm tired of his shit plus the sun is going to be up in a few hours and I have to take cover until night snatch some wheels and get the fuck out of here also it would be nice to hear the news see what the fuck is up and if they've caught on to me yet I'll just get out here pal I tell him and I start to walk towards a small wooden auto court with a gas pump store and what looks like cabins in the back behind the counter is a small blonde I jam a twenty her way and take a room for the next 24 hours yeah that's right sister I like to keep odd hours what's it to you the cabin smells of dust and dead sperm I plop down on the bed combination radio and TV dial around nothing on the radio turn the TV on KTLA News story upcoming about a suspected serial killer haunting the California desert string of commercials I wait pictures of bodies being removed from places that look familiar yet strange removed like looking through a filter the TV says the person they're after has committed three murders the FBI now in on the case fearing the killer has fled across state lines I laugh I only wish I had fled I've been trying to get the fuck out of here for the last forty-eight hours the chopper is up the roads are watched all we can do now is wait we're standing in front of a map of the lower half of the state in an air conditioned trailer on the edge of the desert the insides white new bright taxpayer's dollars bought it we better use it make it work nail this creep so far nothing every bit of evidence collected gone over and over she keeps pounding on the door and crying I open it taker her in my arms she tries to hit me small balled up fists I hug her close take her hand pull her towards the couch reach underneath shove the brown envelope in her hands go ahead read it then see what you

think about me her eyes scan the pages I turn my head I've
done it now we always want what we can't have I made my
choices long ago the house the car the kids never to be this
may be as close as I'll get to any of it if I were her I'd call the
heat rat me out save a politician's life who's going to die she
puts the envelope down stares at me now you know I say
sorrow leaks out of my soul like sap from a tree dark sick
dying she reaches out holds my hands I don't care she says I
don't care I love you why I don't know I think it's because you
make me feel safe wanted needed I'm going to die I tell her
how do you know she asks no one can make this hit and get
out alive no matter how good they are and I'm fucking great
for a junkie been doing it since I was a kid have to go pick up
my equipment get it ready now that you know you'll have to
come turn the TV off and lay back on the bed wish I had a
bottle can't sleep fucking sun's to bright thoughts of going up
to the office and asking about a place to get something to
drink no description how are they going to get me my name
didn't even come up possibly they know it's me and are watching every move I make fucking paranoia setting in Christ got
to cool it and get a bottle then it hits me I grab my duffel bag
pull it open small bottle of downers should I or shouldn't I
would it be safe to lay here a drug induced reptile defenses
down I got to sleep I pop two and my body sags under the
drug eyelids sliding down dreamy state relaxed skulls and faces
float before my eyes I know it's my head I give into it drift off
softly the snake uncoils I walk a lonesome road why can't you
love anyone but yourself Mom yells at me because I can't love
him I try to yell she doesn't or won't hear me and keeps yelling teeth clenched white I'm small trying to reach up to the
Helms Bakery truck made of white hardwood with drawers of
doughnuts I pick two chocolate ones try to hand the money to
the man dressed in white it's my Stepfather the son of a bitch
laughs and keeps the money refusing to give me change my
Mom screaming about bringing home change I've been set up
again I run down the hall she comes after me yelling what did
you do with the change did you steal it lose it she asks a black
belt in her hand grabs me by the hair and tries to hit me he
stands in the doorway laughing it was then he knew he'd kill
him first chance he got rage stacked ready to burn like logs in
a fire of a crazy locomotive instead of stopping she keeps
hitting the young child who is twisting and turning in her hands

trying to work free while the older man laughs the sound of
leather on flesh and the older man's laughing laughing laughing I jerk awake for a second I don't know where I am I roll
off the bed hunker down between the roll and the wall my
eyes lock on the cheap carpet faded and tacked down body
count takes another jump found the motel clerk dead put another mark on the map no pattern to this guy's actions no
description no nothing can only hope he screws up and leaves
us something nothing to do except sit and wait every lead
being followed every tip being followed where is this guy if
we only knew what he looked like what if he were a cop no
can't think that way have to put my mind onto better things
phone rings I hear her voice agree to meet her at the same
place her talk has color in it dark rich a touch of ash the
timber makes me shake with her it's so easy to push the rest of
the world out I can see her naked body a reddish tint to her
makes me hungry and makes me wonder what she sees in me
in an hour I'll find out she walks in front of me and steps on
the escalator into Grand Central we go to a row of lockers at
the end of a deep concrete tunnel I gently guide her my right
hand touching her arm both of us quiet life's a fucking mess
people pass us right and left makes me want to jump out of
my skin and into there's I should got to stop talking shit it'll be
better when it's over I hope she can keep her mouth shut
about this because if she can't I'll have to kill her in fact I
know I'm going to have to cancel her I don't want to but I
have no choice no one can know if I have any chance of
living through this it's like watching TV and wishing you were
in the show so you could run off the set and disappear leaving
behind the fucking mess you've created for yourself turning
the next thing you know she's swimming in your shit up to
her neck and you stand ankle deep shrugging your shoulders
wondering how the fuck you ended up where you are not
because you wanted to end up any place thanks to taking one
step after another and living your life you walk into it blind-
folded your eyes pop open and before you know it she'll be
dead your rotten stench on her breath and you can't see the
point to any of it only God knows it's his cruel fucking game
he makes the rules and then the rules change and there's never
a way out except one and most of us won't take that option
we want a fucking test drive beforehand and it doesn't work
that way got to get myself together I crawl onto the bed swing

my legs over and go to my bag out with some more of the
neon driver it burns my nose top of my head sparkles and
crackles take another snort oh yeah we're together now where's
my baby Gloria dial the phone credit card number given hello
Gloria baby it's me what do you mean who is me you dumb
fucking cunt who do you think me is I'm sorry baby I'm sorry
listen I need to talk to you what do I want I want to talk about
life and death and killing and rage and getting even and sex
and for what I'm fucking paying just listen to what I have to
say I've told you I don't have to pay for it so why do you keep
bringing it up do you know any men who have to pay for it if
they do they're jerks I'm on the road and I want to talk you
know what I want to talk about we've been over this before
OK OK I'm sorry let's start again do you think sex and death
are the same thing like fucking when you get your nuts off it's
like dying like seeing the final answer do you know what I
mean the motel room is a white Spanish stucco look and the
sun strains to get in she's in the bathroom and my head spins
at the smell of her the last time we were out every guy in the
place was checking her out when I'm away from her I can
think about the two of us in a sensible way when she stands
there and I smell her legs long nipples red tipped erect I'd do
anything she asks she works her way back in bed the covers
hanging on one long reddish leg it's as if an artist spray painted
her skin on with a perfect touch she talks to me about the
murders I listen I don't want to hear and I don't want to answer I don't have a clue angel not a clue whoever is doing this
will slip up and leave us something they always do we have
one of the cars he used and we're going over it it's like this
guy is invisible and nobody is invisible nobody there's a lot of
crap going on out there not in here though so hold me I love
you and I said it like that and she pulled away and said what
did you say I don't know what did I say I said sex is like death
don't you think Gloria that's how I want to go sex then death
because sex and death are both about being born and control
and dying and those things are what we are about fucking and
dying don't you think sitting in a cab headed back to her place
we say nothing to each other the cab driver spots what was
put in the trunk and asks if we're going fishing yeah fishing I
answer we're going fishing in Florida the Keys and our eyes
meet and we know it's a lie we're going killing and I've gotten
this fragile angelic baby involved in this and I don't know of

any way out now having to work on two hits him and now her
and for the first time I don't know if I can put her down and
there has to be a way but there's no way she'll talk if pres-
sured she knows it I know it and the cramps are coming on in
the back of my legs and stomach the monster is hungry I got
to fix and at the same time I look at her and I want her and I
don't want to live and I don't want to die and I do want to run
the cab pulls up to her place I pay carry my tools upstairs and
head for the bathroom nothing is said she knows I know and
we both wish it wasn't what it is some things you can't change
Gloria's a fucking cunt she doesn't get it and possibly I don't
get it either I walk outside the motel room and to a Auggie's
Stop across the highway and buy a bottle of cheap wine meth
almost gone now have to have something to get me through
until it's safe to move again I can't keep popping those downers
it clouds my head and then I have to snort up more shit to get
clear so I can take to the roads again this time going to jack
me a car and get clean the fuck away from here I might want
to fuck up the desk clerk for some bread another idea hold up
cars on the interstate why the fuck not there's never any pigs
if you get far enough out wonder if there's a camping supply
store in this micro dot dump she's in the kitchen making dinner pretending like we're a normal couple I spread the gun
parts out on the coffee table I've always loved the feel and
temperature of precision parts that can kill the texture so pleas-
ing to the touch nothing is said between us I oil and polish the
gun putting it together and breaking it down at one point
aiming the cross hairs at the TV and pretending to shoot one
of the talking heads the euphoria of this run through lasts
about ten seconds and the blues starts to spread like toxic ink
in clear water and the world starts to push on the apartment
walls the reality of what must be done breaking in and invad-
ing taking my head and gut prisoner and I know I'm going to
have to kill her and for the first time I don't know that I can
kill this person because she's shown nothing but kindness to
me and we're connected on the other side of this ill gotten
coin there's the fact that if we get caught she could roll on me
in a second and I'd never live to see a courtroom unless I
walked out and jumped bond now I'm into something I can't
back away from does the little girl die or do I trust her not to
say a word what can she say she doesn't know that much she
calls me to dinner who can eat how many days how many

hours into this thing and nothing and then as if God could hear me the phone rings and we've got a break it's small but it's a break I head downstairs to see what's up we gather in a room chipped paint green color bullet holes in the walls pictures of wanted felons large black Xs drawn through their faces meaning their either dead or in the can doing time I miss the clean atmosphere of the field trailer I lean back and listen a pattern is explained a tip is revealed through the Feds a sex talker on a 900 line has this nut who calls talking of death and sex using stolen plastic and the calls fit the flight pattern starting in L.A. and matching the trail of dead meat across a two state area court order in for a tap we get mobile and start to move this could be what we need get on the horn to the trailer in Victorville give the order to move the command post to San Diego this fuck is not going to slip across the boarder because if he tries we'll be right there waiting to put a cap in his head no camping supply store it fucking figures OK the bullshit is over I'm going to send the front desk geek to meet his sweet Jesus get a ride and get the fuck out I can never remember a time when there wasn't shit and I wasn't in some fucked up tragic situation is it me or does God sit up there and say OK so you made this move now I'll make this one and bang like a gigantic finger that moves one fucking barrier in front of you after another until you know he hates you so why doesn't he kill you well I'm going to cheat him and they aren't going to get me staring out the window I see it and I love it a blue VW Beetle not very fast but easy to steal and good on gas I grab my stuff and walk towards the car in the dark the geek behind the desk will have to wait or maybe it's his lucky day in the car I reach under the steering column the little engine turns over and I'm off hey see God I knocked down one of your barriers figure five hours until sundown and at some point they'll know the car was ripped plenty of time to get into Mexico large office building glass steel most likely built in the late 70's we go to the fifth floor boiler room light activity women in small cubicles talking on headsets I flash the badge I hear bits of sex talk here and there we're led to the one called Gloria by a small man light blue carpet coffee stained and worn down with sick boring swirl pattern one of our group Otto Groke hangs his head over one of the stalls a smile on his face laughing at the sex talk we meet Gloria who isn't Gloria at all but a woman named Judy short and cute in a punk kind of way black hair red nails tiny gold ring in her left nostril we look at each other and I feel a slight buzz she says he calls every couple of nights talks for about a half hour or less and hangs up I ask why she does this kind of work and I get a hostile look she tells me she's working her way through college taking courses in business and art this young woman could bring out the dangerous side in a guy last thing I want to do is sit here night after night listening to her talk dirty and wait for the wacko to call we draw lots the five of us I know Otto wants it the rest of us the two Fed boys the state guy and me we don't want it and when it's done I lose and I get it we set up equipment to listen in the next stall and go to the motel for the night I can't wait to call Ruth the buzz from that little Judy still crawling on my skin done with dinner we decide to walk the streets in the cold and snow anything to get out of the hot stuffy apartment after a block she talks first when this is done or when you're done I know you'll leave will you take me with you I won't say anything how do you tell someone you may not even live through what you're about to do why can't she see it it's because she doesn't understand it even though my experience tells me no my gut says yes I sit her down on a bench the snow falling on her hair and I tell her what I have to do why I have to do it and what may or may not happen a Senator she asks repeating it over and over slowly I watch trying to gage her consensus look I tell her he wanted to play and he didn't do what he promised and now he has to pay off and he won't and they can't let him make that vote and I owe them they have me and I have to pay and now you know and you owe me for if you tell anyone I let my voice trail off ohhhh yeah back on the road this little windup monster making it happen zig zagging down the highway the little sewing machine engine whining away colors of orange and red the heat of the road fuck small towns got to get my shit together was in California now to Arizona I'm starting to act like a desert rat running around in circles got to find my way to Mexico and freedom no more meth left got to stay straight and drive drive drive this is the only time I really feel good stealing cars and driving on the open road it's every man's woody isn't it nothing but shit on the radio dumb ass talk shows and tired rock and roll and the news what news there is they're still searching a four state area for me well I'm right here mother fuckers right here and maybe I'll pull off at the next all night joint gas up and leave a reminder so they'll know exactly who their fucking with and it will help crawling through the dark like a roach headed for hell and taking a lot of folks with me we walk in the snow now she knows what it's about I've done what I know is wrong I've put it out on the line she could narc me out right now and there's not a fucking thing I could do about it I feel her hand take mine warm soft what does it mean or what does it matter I still may have to kill her ten o'clock I sit here listening to Judy slash Gloria talked sex to one male caller after another waiting for our guy to call in and trying to keep my control the buzz is on again between us and I try and think of Ruth I haven't seen her in how many days two three I smell her but the this one in the other cubicle makes the blood run with lust staring at the gray woven material covering the cubical watching the meters jump with solid state sex talk this is crazy are there really this many perverts out there guys so hard up they would sit on a phone talk to a voice and get off on it and yet she makes me want to go around the other side of this partition and slam it in her Christ I've got to get a grip here what about Ruth must hold the line see and feel taste her black hair the two of us the taste of her mouth the little peppermint candies she sucks on I push the hot talk out of my head my eyes bore down hard on those broken white lines the little VW eating up highway miles and spitting them out pushing farther and farther from that fucked up town how long before this car is reported gone pull into a Fina station white and red neon light open twenty-four hours one of these places where the mother fucker who owns it lives in a trailer in the back I ought to torch the whole god damn spot but no I fill up and grab a couple of bags of chips and two six packs pay and hit the road drive drive drive got to stay alive got to call Gloria got to stay in control I yank the steering wheel to the right and the car skids off the road into the dirt the bouncing and swerving like an out of control space capsule I straighten the VW up and get control there's that word again control and the car slides to a stop in the middle of nowhere nothing except desert not a soul around I switch off the engine the interstate is off in the distance cars like crystal lice dart back and forth against the darkness I start walking gun in hand she sits me down in the living room look she says I'm in with you I love you and I'm in with you take me with you and I'll help you no one will even think there

would be a man and a woman the two of us who would think
to search for the two of us I want to cry and can't we kiss the
TV running holding hands like teenagers if we go we go together how do I know she still won't spill or go sloppy on me
at the last second I glance over at her she's fallen asleep on
my shoulder the smell of her close to me both excites and
scares me is this wise she's a good woman but I'll have to
leave options open and kill her if she drifts on me where the
hell is our call how long can I sit hear and listen to her talk
about sucking and fucking and we were joking between calls
and I think she wants it what about Ruth how would I explain
this is a police matter now how to stop a car this is America
where you never stop for someone you don't know because
you might get your ass handed to you on a fucking platter I
stand on the edge of the highway thumb out cars pass right
and left trails of cold air and exhaust I'd like to fucking kill
them the red lights fading into black here's a car stopping I
run to it jump in two young girls driving a late model green
BMW now make a little conversation get a bit down the road
I pull the gun grab the driver by the hair the car zig zags they
scream I yell she pulls the vehicle off the road and into the
desert the car runs for a mile or so on its own until it comes to
a halt nothing darkness like a protective blanket against the
outside world he orders them out of the car the headlights on
he shouts motioning back and forth with a gun the two young
girls stand in front of the vehicle trembling and crying he orders them to strip they stand and cry he hits both of them with
his gun now do it or die they tremble and comply stumbling
out of their clothes what do you mean would I buy you a
drink well it's the least I can do her shift is over and we go to
a small cocktail lounge across the street purples and greens I
ask her how long she's been talking sex and she tells me over
a year do you ever get carried away when you're on the phone
with some of these guys no she says it's like acting we laugh
and drink our beers there's a ring going on I can sense it taste
it smell it see it and I know she can too how much and what
does it take to corrupt each of us for some it's money some it's
women and some murder some it's power aren't they one in
the same is it going to be a woman for me I know I'm edging
towards the line the sun is up and the day burst in through the
window now less than twenty four hours away from the crime
it's our last day together I walk to the bathroom to fix we

should do something special today the smile from the day
quickly fades with the ingestion of the drug and the realiza-
tion there isn't much time left now the old feeling of sadness
kept at bay by the numerous amounts of opiates running
through the system seeps back black and fowl take the money
and split runs through my mind like a thin bloody thread in
one side and out the other it's no option one way or the other
I'll die the I now becomes WE and if things were bad inside
my head three weeks ago now there's a fucking storm going
on I lie down on the bed and examine her delicate fingers the
skin so fine almost translucent with fragile finger tips who
could or would want to kill such a marvelous thing who would
want to trade her life for theirs and in doing so have no life in
return I turn over and try to go back to bed but it's inside me
ticking like a bomb and I know it'll go off and I won't be able
to control it learned behavior hard to unlearn I specialize in
eating my own they stand in the white headlights naked hands
trying to hide the small triangles of hair between their legs he
orders one to lay down in the sand and she drops down crying her long hair chestnut in color hangs on her bare shoulders
the night outlines her body in black she looks like a young girl
playing in the sand maybe at the beach waiting on her boyfriend to come back with hot dogs and fries the sound of
ocean and the wind causing the ends of her hair to dance
there used to be something about the ocean with the salt and
sand and looking off in the horizon or walking down the little
boardwalk at night eating in one of the small fish joints that
use to make him feel good like there was hope of something
anything happening a clean good feeling torn away by progress
people and too much garbage the girl lays in the sand and
waits he orders the other girl to lie down there was a time
when he got high on acid and ran around in the sand and it
was the moon it looked and felt like the moon and there was
nobody out there and the whole coastline was a marvelous
playground and there were women everywhere and they'd
talk and it was that one summer when he got popped for
beating that cunt Lucinda up because she was a cock tease
and he never felt better giving it to her in the ass and beating
the shit out of her sitting in the county jail no one would talk
to him it's crumbling into a pile of garbage strewn with trash
and sick sea gulls and dead pigeons that's why he got out now
the two girls are down in the sand and he points the gun at

them and orders them to perform to make love to each other to do it and do it now and do it slow suck each other's titties and pussy he yells waving the gun the hammer cocked the one with the chestnut hair moves to the other one working her tongue over her friend's nipples and he's hard and thinking of Gloria if she could only see this she'd see he doesn't need a phone call to get what he wants I see the line coming up and I know I shouldn't step across it and I try to step back but it's as if I were being pulled over it by this woman I pay for our drinks tell her good night an awkward pause in the parking lot one of us waits for the other to make a move I drive back to the motel TV on try to call Ruth she's not there leave a message still hot and bothered wondering what it would be like it's OK to wonder isn't it human nature right what's the big deal about sex without love no I'm rationalizing or am I would I sleep with her right now if she'd show up at the door another one on the case and randy as a goat there goes another officer with his tin down the tubes good cop gone bad old story now I'm caught in it is it because I want to be caught or can't help myself am I acting like a man or am I being an animal she wakes and hugs me and stretches like a fine lean cat the air is fine and for the first time we really make love and I'm lost in her and the monster whatever it is the fucking monster that makes me turn on a dime and destroy in order to live is now deep under layers of her skin disarmed and bathed in her love and fucking tears start I can't recall the last time I cried and I know we've both got to get through this and get clear of it the junk the violence all of it never wanting this moment to stop I lay on top of her inside her never wanting to come out there is no job to pull there is no living or dying there's only this and we both work to prolong the moment as long as we can the two girls are trying to go through the motions their bodies and shadows move in the headlights and darkness he moves with them and some place Gloria is here and she's is with them too and when the girls can go on no longer their crying and whimpering getting louder he walks up behind the one on the left and puts a bullet in her skull forcing brains and blood to splatter on the other girl like a bucket of red paint and she gets up and starts to to run her body covered in blood and bone he shoots her three times she tumbles the dry ground and sand moist with her body fluids he loads their bodies in the trunk of their car and leaves them tracking back to the Beetle and hitting the interstate again hoping to clear the state line by morning this in Arizona out of Arizona in California out of California hopping back and forth like a jacked up drug infested insect is getting thin his nerves starting to show beneath the skin eyes floating in hollowed out sockets moving from one dark place to the next resting only at sunup we lay in her bed and nothing is said between us she reaches over and holds my hand her fingers cold and soft they say there is someone for everyone I had often heard it never believed it the only thing I ever thought was for me was the spike or was it because I never let it happen or was it because the part of a person that lets them love and care doesn't fit with a person who sends people to see sweet Jesus and now this woman has shattered the myth I'm going to take you someplace I've never taken anyone today are you game to go she nods yes a smile on her oval face and large green eyes and I want to fuck her over and over again when the phone rings I know it's bad news I pick it up another killing two girls found stuffed in the trunk of a car off the interstate two souls gone among the cactus heat and flies nothing to do but wait for this monster's call and keep my hands to myself I kill most of the day walking in town examining shop windows and try-ing to keep myself together before another night of sex talk the time runs like a crawl place three calls to the office noth-ing on the girls other than it appears to be the work of the same asshole who did the others now loose in the desert some-where we have no clues except the calls and the plastic he stole I try to keep count of the people he's taken out and can't recall not sure which is loading up first my head or my crotch to much time in the day on this gig the buildings are run down and gray with soot and dirt the grass brown and there's graffiti everywhere you look we climb out of the cab it's cold dismal she holds my hand tight the hallway is littered with trash el-evator is enough to scare the shit out of anyone paint chipped scratched away smell of urine gang signs here and there it lurches to the fifth floor we get out down a dank hallway I knock on the door of apartment number 7 he comes to the door peeks though the chain it's me Pops I say with a friend we're inside it's tiny and smells of age and dead flesh nothing is said I open the conversation how you doing Pops OK he answers back why did you come Bobby and who's this with you one of your one night whores Pop please can't we just no

we can't he spits back she squeezes my hand I thought well
you thought wrong he says same old bitter bastard never chang-
ing his bones and heart made of ash look Pop you need any
money wouldn't take it if you gave it to me a small motel store
gas station coming up on the left bright in the darkness of the
open land its sign in the shape of a huge green square with a
flashing pan of gold set in the middle late night check in I ring
the bell come on mother fucker a thin hard scrabble woman
comes to the window I give her one of the stolen cards hopes
she doesn't run it and she doesn't dumb bitch over to the store
get a couple of pints and a couple of sixes packages of candies and cassette tapes on display by the cash register inside
my head I'd love to smash every fucking thing in this place
and I'd fucking do it if I could right now I got other things on
my mind get my drink and check in my room carry a bottle
with me in the shower I love this hot water and cold drink like
the difference between day and night makes me wonder how
many shit heads are out there on the hunt for me here I am
warm water drink the whole planet a killing field drink it straight
never going to go to the joint again the one question never
asked why didn't I kill my old man with his pussy bullshit he
still breaths I ought to show up at his place and pistol whip
his head into a lump of bone and blood let's see who gets the
last laugh in this life the cock sucker his laughing hyena face
and soft woman like flesh hanging from his face I'd like to
carve it off piece by piece I throw the bottle against the shower
wall the glass shatters off the dirty yellow tile surface I dance
in blood shards of glass cut my feet streaks of blood like jet
trails find their way to the drain and disappear I walk on my
heels out of the shower fall on the bed I take her hand we
leave nothing said between us down the elevator into the
waiting cab back to the city the ride long painful and silent I'd
kill the old man the same way he killed everything else but
what good would it do to put him out of his misery let him rot
in that stinking shit pile he calls a house a house is not a
house until it's a home yeah sure the sun is down night is here
I sit at the equipment I don't know why I tell Judy but tonight's
the night he'll call I feel it and he's murdered two girls and
he'll call it's his pattern first two hours two old man from Iowa
one a banker the other a priest I try to keep from cracking up
never heard a man have an orgasm while moaning hail Mary
God is full of grace take another drink see what gives I chase

the whiskey with beer bitter taste in my mouth well life is fucking bitter yah yah yah I should call the cunt Gloria tell her I've had two today how many has she had why do people drink it doesn't taste worth a shit only fucks you up what you're reaching for is the fuck up the place where it's safe and warm and whatever your head makes it will even make the fucking dead dance I drive my fist through the wall knuckles bloody I don't feel a thing pick the phone up the whole ritual a turn on hey Gloria it's your twisted fucked up sick telephone no sex lover let me talk to you baby it's him she tells me over her headset I pick up the phone and call downtown they start the trace I roll tape nod for her to go ahead I knew he'd call Gloria it's your blood thirsty sugar daddy baby how have you been yes I did the two girls I had two today can you top that I told you baby death is sex no better way to get your rocks off where am I oh no baby I'm on the road got to sell sell sell you know the American way and all what's wrong baby something's wrong I can sense it I motion for her to keep him going another couple of seconds come on Judy God damn it no I don't want any fucking sex I'm going to come there and kill you come to think of it me and you together your final moments of pain and suffering how about it baby hey I know something's wrong and if you've sold me out I'm going to come there and kill you for sure understand how an animal senses it feels knows it its fur goes up on its back and it smells someone or something I smell it on you you cunt and you know what I'll bet it's the cops I tell her to keep him talking we are so close come on baby tears welling up and spilling over running down her cheeks I know it's the cops and you're dead bitch I slam down the phone gulp a full take of whiskey chase it with beer my head spins I'm going to off the cunt forget about the border I have to make a stop to see the bitch then I'll hook it south he hung up did we get it I shout over the phone almost he was calling somewhere along the California Arizona border could have even been hell no better off than before will he call back I conference call with the brass stay another day and see what gives he claims he's going to kill this girl here so if he starts in that direction we use Judy as the bait like the movies I tell them except with real people I leave her outside to wait and I go in the public rest room to fix put the healing syrup in my vain the warmth moves up me like a sick black flower petals blooming among the stink through my body I start to nod not the place struggle to my feet outside she helps me inside the movie I nod on her shoulder she could give me up right now stop the movement of history the killing of a Senator oooh I spoke the word never say it out loud she tells me to stop mumbling I embrace the dark for its quiet and peaceful comfort pictures expand and contract on the screen my mind fixates on the sound of the projector mixed with the sound of the movie the world is full of movies I can't grab hold of the film spilling out everywhere unyielding dark and sharp around the edges I'm in my body buried deep somewhere through layers of dark thought a tiny candle only a flicker it's decided our man may try to show to grab Judy so myself Groke and one Fed and State are assigned to stay and help the one bullet dicks in this town make sure nothing happens to her and also be ready in case the mope shows his face I leave Groke to watch think and hit the interstate back to Angel town to pick up clothes and get a wire on Ruth haven't seen her in a awhile I long for her smell and warmth want to run to her to hide from Judy and the wrong I know I'm going to do brings back the old thing about love and what it really is does anyone know what it is except a word and there's nothing to say about it because its been said so many times my Mother and Father knew it for 40 years fiddle with the radio and force my mind to jump to this freak we're hunting gut tells me he'll show don't they always wish I knew what drives this type does he want to make a statement is it in his head a part missing the drive is long nothing fast food and gas stations dirt and brown grass wide long oil and exhaust stain runs underneath the car rubber coats the road things change and then things never change times passes and then it never passes idle thoughts idle time what's murder like to do it to want to do it everyone thinks about it few carry it out what's it like to kill and never look back there is this part of everyone this bell or warning sign goes off you know things aren't right and nothing you can do will make it right I know the cunt Gloria has sold me out or done something I can tell man I know man I know I need something anything a snort a shot this drink is fucking me up deep burning fire inside hot and driving got to score somewhere and if any mother fucker gives me shit I'll split them apart in one fucking zip and wash my hands in their dope dealing scum sucking blood nothing white lines and black road for hours now nothing to score out there fucking peanut butter logs what bullshit no wonder this country is fucked up whenever I see one of those fucking Stuckey's all I think about is him and her and me summer time travel always too cheap to buy a fucking thing so why the fuck would he drag me in there in the first place for aren't kids supposed to have candy not me and I knew inside he was laughing about it laughing and laughing the cock sucking pervert hours and hours of ridding in the fucking car nothing except Mexican music blaring from the radio him and her in their own world the other three there with them and me by myself like I was absent invisible too bad I'll never get a chance to fuck them over like they did me he had them gathered in the living room lined up against the rock and concrete fireplace hands clasped behind their heads they begged and asked why and it made him boil with anger this was the reason he had to kill them they would never ever recognize what they had done to him never see it or hear it or feel it he shot the old man first blowing his glasses off a wide splotch of blood smeared over the rocks the bridge of his nose shattered splinters of bone blowing where there had once hung Christmas stockings then he shot the rest leaving them to struggle to hang on to life in their own blood and filth strangling on the very fluids that once kept them alive the headlines read HE KILLED HIS ENTIRE FAMILY now the headlines are going to read he killed everyone except his family well that's how the coin comes down pulling down a gym bag I stuff some clothes in no time to even take a shower call Ruth leave a message on her machine the sound of her ruby red voice makes me lonely for those legs the smell of her the touch of her I know what's going to happen if I let it go got to walk a straight line bag packed back in the car and back on the interstate down towards San Berdoo I push it to make the first round of nightly sex calls from the lonely and twisted hope Groke is OK the traffic is a killer this time of the day sun screaming through the windshield I flip on the KFWB news station want to hear someone talk the movie over she helps me from the theater we walk along the street I want to say something some shit about if we get through this I'll clean up we'll get out of this fucking clty start again go somewhere where there's sunshine no gray buildings and yellow signs bathed in a sick dim light I can't bring myself to say it I know it's not true not any of it if I don't die from a bullet I'll die from a needle and I know I have to kill her or kill myself first the thought of skipping with the cash and the stash zips across my head again they would find us and we'd be fucked she pulls my hand and we duck into a small pub dark cool shimmering greens and reds beer signs wink hello golden yellowish color we sit at the bar she orders a couple of beers I have to surge out of this stupor and get control no macho bullshit in here no cops no drawing attention this is out of my norm right before I'm going to hit someone I lay very low and stay low don't want to bump into some snitch let the word get out to the snitches I'm in town I keep my head down and drink with one hand and hold her hand with my other hand nothing is said nothing need be said she orders us another the TV casts shadows and light over the small room the sound turned down low faces and bodies going through the motions I think I love you she whispers I don't answer just take another drink sundown and I score a couple of bottles of Turkey and get a room at the Prospector's Motel a room at the end in the back and I start to drink and drink hard I'm restless and can't sit still a dozen fucking freak ideas start to pop out at me like snakes out of a wicker basket should I be driving at night and laying low in the day no that's what they would expect how long has it been without any drift man seems like a fucking generation how many dead bodies left behind eyes keep staring at me through bloody sockets I keep drinking got to stop this shit I'd like to take a fire ax to the walls of this hell hole chop my way into the room next door and fucking kill every prick in there bits of plasterboard everywhere in dusty piles sections of wallpaper torn hanging here and there and I'd keep at it until I had chopped through the whole fucking place I take another belt the sting of the liquid floods my stomach and works to coat my nerves like watering down an electrical fire after three beers we bundle up and start to walk in the dark every hour I spend with this woman the commitment grows deeper and I try and pull away I want to live not die by some cop's bullet I have to figure a way out not only for me for both of us if I could get to a small hospital somewhere and get clean we could have something suppose I could get us through this whole thing alive would you want to go with me I ask she nods her head and squeezes my hand I already told you I did she says eyes big sad I turn my head so she won't see the tears the fucking tears I haven't cried since I was a fucking kid man

I'm in deep bits of my flesh and soul ripped away like having
yourself dragged bloody over a gravel road the rocks tearing
at you bit by bit and the confusion is enough makes you want
to put a fucking pistol to your head right now the temptation
of not making the job dangling around out there in the dark
the thoughts of running and always running stacking up knowing if I run I'll always run they'll never let me walk Spanish on
this deal she and I would forever be trying to stay alive as
long as I'm hittin' I'm still shitin' I remember I use to say it
over and over again like a chant or a dance like both killing
and swimming to a shoreline that never appears on account of
once you start you can't stop until it gets you or kills you and
the higher ups own you from your ass to your scalp and they'll
cut you down any time they don't need you and it's worse
when your strung out one drop of the word and you can't get
shit on or off the street I have to get the concept about skipping out of my head in Vacca Hills I pull the car in and get set
for another night of sex talk and maybe a phoner from our
boy Groke seems relived to see me and hits the door I sit in
the cubicle and listen and listen and try to stop thinking about
the woman on the other side and how much I want her most
of the callers are boring tonight the same thing the only thing
funny is the age of some of them including the old man who
wanted Gloria to read from the bible while he jerked off I
nearly cracked up and she had to tell me to be quiet a couple
of times and finally I had to get up and go stand over by the
drink box I was laughing so hard sometimes I sit and think
how crazy this is and why after what I saw with my old man
and his frustration trying to turn the world around as Mom
used to say why did I joined the force in the first place did I
do it because I wanted to or did I do it out of a sense of duty
I sit back down and put on the headphones the calls come
through from across the country credit card numbers taken
sex talk given the TV set comes on and I scan the channels
hugging the bottle in my lap searching for anything about me
and there's nothing or I thought there was fucking nothing
until the story appears three state manhunt for West's newest
mass murderer and rapist where do they get this mass murderer shit from my leg starts working I take another hard pull
from the bottle if they think their going to pop me they can
fuck off I haven't even started to fuck people over yet and the
great thing is they keep trying to get a peek at me at night and

I keep moving in the daylight then at night then in the daylight I'm not going to fucking hide like a cockroach fuck 'em
and yes I have to call the cunt Gloria with her pig buddies
listening in man you talk about fucking someone up I'm going
to have her and then I'm going to kill her and I'll do it right
under the nose of her fucking cop boyfriends sex and death as
one no ending and no beginning I walk outside in the night to
a pay phone on a steel pole under a yellow light I know I
can't talk long I pull another piece of hijacked plastic from my
back pocket and punch in the numbers the cunt better be
there the phone rings it's our guy I put the headphones on
recorder running signal for them to transfer him in hope they
get a line on him this time so Gloria are you sitting there with
your cop friends are you sucking them off baby let me tell you
what it's like to have sex in the midst of panic and death it's
like meeting the Devil and smelling his fowl breath rolling in
the flames of searing desire and you know what baby I'm
going to show you what it's like oh yeah no more strange for
me I'm saving it for you and me and the Devil I'm coming
baby so wait for me and I'll take your cop friends along too
the line goes dead I call the downtown exchange did we get it
yes a phone booth in California Arizona call to short no trace
fucking lot of good its going to do us Judy runs from her
phone cubicle crying for the first time I really wouldn't mind
killing this asshole the thought moves through my head like a
storm front and then clears there ain't no sunshine nothing
harsh light in bands of white and yellow it's the morning of
the job no way to put it off now I move to the bathroom and
fix to get a jump on the day it's hard my hand shakes and I
almost drop the brown encrusted spoon somehow I must have
picked up a staff infection my right arm is swollen and tender
at the main artery and it hurts at the joint when I move it not
a good indicator why do I think this day is going to suck or am
I setting myself up for this true I have to kill a guy that's never
been a problem in the past I might even have to kill two people
and the chances are red fucking hot I'm going to die too now
who in their right mind would think it's going to be a bad day
the central question is how to spend these last hours the shot
not being until tonight I walk back to the bedroom she sleeps
and I want to cry things were fucked up from the start now
there worse he picks up a pillow and handles it flips it over a
few times tossing it in the air thinking not thinking and then

plunges it down over her head she wakes and he senses the panic building in her body and she kicks and he pushes harder putting his body into it fighting struggling for air the will to live he never tires of observing the will to live he becomes a cold distant observer watching another's hands he pushes harder leaning his weight on her she fights on until there's no fight left she's gone without a word escaping her lips like a well programmed machine he pulls the covers over her showers packs his things removes any finger prints gets his gear and heads for the subway he'll ride it most of the day staying underground and lost until it's time because in the end we are what we are he killed her so he could live there's no turning back now so let them try and bust me I hang up the phone and walk back to the room take a hard hungry pull from the bottle the warm liquid eating my insides and dulling my head killing time until sunup I lay back and my eyes walking the wallpaper noticing every shitty crack and peeled spot faded patterns plastered up long ago with good intentions now old like life long after I'm gone the wall paper will still sit and watch silently while the fucking killing drinking loneliness goes on some dumb ass traveling salesman on his knees in the small hours asking God why his life is so fucked up why he's so lonely working his ass off while his old lady is banging his next door neighbor her naked body pale in the light wrapped around another man and what can he do about it nothing except hit the road and make those sales calls and ask where's the Christ Child when I need him and will he save me and turn things around stop the throbbing pain in my heart I take a copy of the bible from a flimsy wooden night table and it's a Gideon and take it in the bathroom pour bourbon on it and flick a match it burns and it's what I think of the whole fucking thing the flames eat the fine paper and the thick cover sizzles and pops and it reminds me of a cloudy rainy day childhood fooling with matches because there was nothing else to do and taking a twenty dollar bill out of my Mother's wallet and burning it up for no reason or was there a reason to get back at him for the stinking shit he poured on me day after day so now I spend the rest of my life trying to get even his fucking face inside my head no matter what I do he won't leave I've killed him a thousand times and he won't die he laughs like the others laugh those cops and the cunt Gloria well she won't laugh when I fucking cut her uterus out and nail it to a wall flies and ants nibbling at the exposed organ wet with blood her crying stops and she sits back down in her cubicle nothing is said and we both sit there the emotion of complete tenderness swells up and washes over me I'm sad the whole world is sad one of the three of us is going to have to die and I know it won't be her one of us will have to if only we knew something anything about this prick he might be out there right now waiting watching no this line of thinking is not going to get me anywhere let's think it out he's out there not here and when he comes here I'm going to arrest him and kill him only if I have to this point is important if I act like him I might as well be him and in some way we're all like him I pat my gun in its shoulder holster I'm ready I think I'm ready it's time and I check my watch again to make sure I get off the train car and take the escalator up walk to the stairs and out in the street everything is normal for this city if they only knew this is one of the parts I love I walk among them knowing someone is going to die and only I know and it helps push away the sadness of her dying of the whole rotten mess when I reach South Broadway I go to the building named in the instructions and take the elevator to the top the key to unlock the door to the roof is there above dirty white molding running the length and width of the door I'm on the roof in no time and start to set up behind a huge electric sign the letter R perfect for my gun barrel I smoke and wait for the motorcade to pass by listening to a small radio with an ear plug I monitor the Senator's progress careful to make sure no one comes up behind me I tune to WINS the news station and listen to the traffic reports and the time and temp nothing to do now smoke and wait getting up I walk to the roof door and make sure it's locked no need to arouse any suspicion with only one way up and one way down I'll have to move quick after I get the shots off escaping is all I think about can't stay in this room any longer can't sit still I walk outside and find myself walking towards the center of town I know this is wrong and I should stay in the room and keep quiet I can't help myself it must be anticipation of the kill my legs are like high voltage wires they want to snap and dance how could anyone live in a place like this and what the fuck do people do here I spot a small biker bar and go inside it's dark and cool beer signs blink in shinny red and blue fluids a few guys playing pool under a harsh light pinball machines in the corner I order a beer and a shot to try

and cool out what I wouldn't give for some crystal my face
stares back at me from a long mirror behind the bar I look like
shit heavy bags under my eyes like two soft purses stapled to
my skin I need to finish my drink and get the fuck out I don't
need the trouble and somehow no matter what I do it always
finds me a couple of more shots inside me I walk over to an
Injun in a tall black hat and sit down he looks up at me from
his beer our eyes meet he knows what I want without saying
it he knows I'm speed crazy like a fucking rat with its head
bashed in I don't even think about things and what I'm doing
it's automatic and we sit and say nothing two beers sit and
stare he's not going to kill you I tell her he won't get near you
Groke's a good cop and I'm a good cop the State and Fed
boys are not such good cops she smiles they'll be there too we
drink in silence then she starts to tell me how she ended up
talking dirty to hundreds of men in North America for a living
it seemed like a good idea at the time and an easy way to turn
a buck she didn't plan to do it forever only for a little while
you get real fond of the money and then it becomes tough to
say no and the next thing you know a couple of months becomes a year and you stop asking yourself what the hell you're
doing you do it and the calls mean nothing you've heard the
jokes a thousand miles away the ugly woman doing her nails
and reading while she's faking fucking a chump on the phone
getting him off we both laugh if you had a boyfriend how
would he know your mind wasn't a thousand miles away and
you were faking it I never fake that she says laughing yeah but
how would your boyfriend know I ask he'd know she says
with a smile the tension builds around the table and gets thick
I poke at my drink it's there neither of us wanting to pick it up
maybe I'll call you one of these nights why she says I'm sure
you have no trouble getting the real thing to see if you recognize my voice and we both laugh the Injun and I step behind
a couple of parked cars don't try and donkey fuck me Red
Man or I'll chew your guts up for a snack and drink your
blood he gets it I've been there and back and we deal a small
bag I cop it scurry back to the motel room like an animal with
a catch inside I turn on the TV there's a talk show on hosted
by some fat fucking woman I can shoot or snort this shit and it
better be good or I'll burn the fucking flesh off that Red Man I
tap out a small amount of powder lay it in a line and snort it
the drug kicks my head oh man I am on now I step in the

shower with a bottle of whiskey oh Gloria I'm coming to kill
your warm pussy I'm coming to send you to the angels my
dick grows hard I stroke it because of the drug I can't come
I'm gripped by my own madness and I love the warmth of it
stepping out of the shower I sit on the bed watching the TV
waiting for night to come and the feel of my Gloria's warm
flesh gone cold like marble in a winter graveyard giant helium
balloons in the shape of cartoon characters float by people
dressed in reds and greens the motorcade is under way I scan
for his limo crowds of people milling around and waiting I
glimpse through the scope the cross hairs stop on a young
blond girl standing eating a bag of popcorn I could squeeze
the trigger right now end her life and she doesn't even know it
I play with the idea of putting a slug right through her pretty
white teeth that's not what I'm here for and I put the gun
down and scan the area with a small pair of binoculars no one
in sight I don't think anyone knows I'm even here this could
work out OK if I'm cool I wipe my palms on my pants and
wait the radio continues to bark color and commentary in my
left ear I pull out a photo of the car I'm looking for and the
Senator and I see the car make the turn slowly coming my
way I act on reflexes alone have to put unnecessary facts and
emotions out my head and concentrate on the fucking target
the car slowly making its way up the wide street crowds lined
on both sides cheering people happy and smiling the conversation is at a dead end I feel uneven how is someone supposed
to feel listening to this woman talk about sex for four hours
and now alone with her in a bar my motel room there like a
throbbing beacon calling and begging I can see the room in
my head the two of us naked on the bed Ruth standing there
crying watching yet I can't stop hungry to make words stand
up and dance with action we walk to the car inside we're
close and I can smell her every cell in my body alive and on
hot alert we start to drive I know where we're going and so
does she nothing is said how about a drink I ask one for the
road for the road she asks with a raised eyebrow yeah I say
throat dry inside the room he kicks the door shut and they kiss
pushing their way to the bed and she starts talking to him like
she's at work this is what you wanted isn't it she asks he rolls
away from her face moist with tears and sadness no he whispers what I want is you he says not who you play every night
on the phone he can't believe he's saying this he feels stained

with shame and want she's in his arms the head of gray hair moves in between the cross hairs I am The Angel Of Death I mumble a kind of ritual game I play my finger senses the trigger the car moves she stands and takes off her clothes letting them drop to the floor she has a bit of a tummy her legs are short and fine she comes to him on fours from behind she hisses I see his eyes and teeth he's smiling and waving his arm shifts in and out of my sights in splashes of dark blue yes the right suit for every occasion perhaps I'll do a double winger he holds her waste and pulls her to him they struggle in pinks and browns flesh on flesh his cock stiff and wet a cement mixer of flesh and fluids she moans and thrusts her buttocks back at him the gun kicks a bit and one shot rips his arm tearing at his flesh blood in mid air like red rain drops the gun bucks again and his head explodes the whole front caving in I wheel the sight around and fire at a young boy in the crowd hitting him in the chest he falls backwards people panic I break down the gun wipe off any prints and stuff it down an exhaust duct there are no numbers on it so they can't trace it I run for the door have to haul ass now he tries to take her from the front and they fight to see who has dominance she tries to overpower him I run down flight after flight of stairs the sound of helicopters circling above the roof bounces off the concrete walls I pull my nine out of my coat hold it at my side only two more flights to the lobby he lets her win put it in my mouth she demands he sits up on his knees and she takes him licking his balls in the lobby there's panic confusion people cops everywhere I pocket the hardware and walk towards the door someone calls to me I ignore them and keep walking they call again and I go through the revolving doors to the street two men follow it hits me and I want to laugh it's like the movies they either saw me coming out the door or I've been set up in either case those two men will not go home tonight he tries can't hold it anymore and comes bits of him dribble down her lips and chin they collapse together and say nothing panic hits him over what he's done the sun burns yellow and sad on the fucking road again a meth high the little VW fights the wind and keeps moving this is so fucking amazing these dicks know I'm out here yet they can't catch me and I keep going even in this boosted set of wheels somewhere down the line I'll have to dump this thing because the longer I drive the chances are I'll get nailed I got to keep to myself talk to no one I can't blow this I'm going to have a day and a half with this rotten little cunt Gloria guilt creeps up from inside him and is coated in silence what's the matter she asks nothing he tells her she knows better his arm around her lacks enthusiasm he's never understood how this worked you want it before hand so bad you'd do almost anything and then when you have it you don't want it anymore and you try hard to fight the sensation of being crowded by guilt and remorse represented by the body naked in bed next to you there's nothing wrong he tells her again you see there's this I get it she says have some real live sex with a voice that thrills thousands of horny old men a little something to tell your copper buddies no that's not it he tries to explain she bolts out of bed and pulls on her clothes the door slams shut and he lays there calm the smell of her still on his skin the phone rings and rings again people are everywhere on the street good cover if only I didn't have these two pigs after me I step back in a doorway and slide a blade out from under my pant leg the first one arrives and I nail him with my fist he falls knees first to the ground and I make a fast surgical cut to the Adam's apple leaving a curtain of dark blood running along his throat like a sick smile the second one brings it on and I stick a blade in his gut and pull up using all my strength his eyes burn into mine a look of shock he falls backwards hits a newspaper box and stops sprawled in the street before a bystander can say anything I light foot it and go down into a train tunnel taking three steps at a time the tunnel smells like shit and I feel better once the train pulls away I pull into San B and now to a phone booth at an Arco station drop a couple of coins in the slot the booth is tight and the glass scarred with scratch graffiti a dull voice comes on the line I raise my voice trying to speak over the traffic yes this is Captain Spangler from the special task force I need to know where to set up extra surveillance in the phone sex murder case and the only number I seem to have is this one a pause on the line the voice comes back we're not allowed to give out that information sir who did you say you were I slam down the phone my fingers tap and drum the meth driving me like cheap gasoline exploding and pushing the pistons in my head and then I remember it the small print on the bottom of the screen TV Orion Telecommunications Inc I dial and get the number from information and could you tell me what street that's on just to make sure I have the right

name and then I get it 2123 Mar Vista Way and it's mine and I
have her now I abandon the car for the cops to find after
taking a good long leak on the seats and steering wheel fuck it
let them find it and see what they can come up with if I had to
bet I'd bet they won't find the poor creature for days until
someone calls and reports it the sun starts to dip tonight will
be the night I check into the Del Mar a small motel quiet slow
room in the back now the fucking game commences I lay out
three victory lines the powder jacks my head I can see it in
World Weekly News he always hid in small motels using back
rooms for his base of sick operations well they can blow me
because I feel sharp as a steel blade every nerve on high alert
ready for flesh and conquest her voice comes across the wires
like silk and I get a shiver in my gut oh Ruth I want to yell I
love you and I've done something so wrong will you understand can you forgive me instead I try to stop the shaking and
listen does my voice sound funny it's nerves only nerves honey
I'll see you soon yes I love you and I miss you I sit paralyzed
the smell still there why do we have to want everything then
find out we only want some things into the shower tonight
might be the night the thought sends another rumble in the
gut the whole thing out there coming like a brick wall you can
side step it yet you'll never avoid it off the train I climb the
stairs to street level eyes darting here there everywhere nothing no one around I might have pulled this fucker off next
question how do I get out of the city why didn't I think of it
never thought I would get this far can't go back to her apartment shit got to find a place to fix legs feeling funny I duck
into a coffee shop men's room pull my kit out got to get juiced
enough to stay well so I can pull my ass out of this only choice
I figure while hitting a vein is lay some balls out there and go
to the airport book a ticket to Madrid and take my chances try
and get well now do I go by taxi train or bus walking in the
telephone boiler room I take my place by the phone and re-
cording equipment she says nothing to me and I want to say
everything to her explain why and what happened and how
you can get carried away and you reach a point and you can't
turn back no matter how much you try and no matter how
wrong it is anything to wipe the stain and then I get what he
must be into out there roaming around now headed this way
too deep in too far to turn back sex and killing no room for
those who want to dance on the rim of the bowl either you're

in up to your chest or you're out he has no choice has to come here and die to finish what he started back in L.A. and continued through the deserts of California and Arizona like I knew once I started with her I would finish it by sleeping with her oh I never said it out loud the buzz was there ok now I'm steady to the airport how to get there I got bread but I'll bet they expect me to try that so I'll go to the Port Authority bus station and take a hound down to Laredo, Texas cross into Mexico and fly from there he rolls down his sleeve comes out of the stall washes his hands pulls on his coat he notices a man standing next to him he sense something is wrong he can't put his finger on why he turns to walk out excuse me he says bumping into him the pain shoots through his gut slicing at him like a harsh musical note amplified a thousand times his hands grab for his stomach there's blood warm sticky it's his oh what the fuck how could this have happened he gasps tries to focus on the tile and dirt on the floor to get a focus on things he squeezes his eyes shut and opens them pulls himself up there's blood everywhere he's a mess for God's sakes I'm a fucking jumble of blood guts bleeding like a pig he cries out gets on his feet he stands eying the man who assaulted him and he reaches in his coat pocket and fires off a round hitting his assailant in the cheek bone blowing away half his face in one big blood blur smear if I'm going you're going too mother fucker he hisses leaning against the door he's dizzy wet he can't feel himself crash forward through the bathroom door on to the floor of the restaurant people scream move around him he can't make out what their saying no pain no nothing dark cold so fucking cool he's numb it's like what he thought it would be a smile crosses his cracked and death dry lips in the back-seat of a cab they'll never be watching for that I pay the driver out right here across the street by a phone booth this is going to be almost as cool as getting high what the fuck I take a few booster snorts the powder clinging to the fine oil of pink human fingertips money in the phone the call comes through she starts talking tape rolling hey baby how are you my fucking cunt how are you do you know where I am baby let me tell you where I am I can see you right now and I'm going to have you so many different ways and then baby I'm going to kill you hear me think about it smearing the walls with your blood and maybe you know what maybe I'll make your pig friends roll in it and slip and slide in it and I'll tell them how warm you were when I did you and how you made noises and struggled and how it only made me want to kill you more my tough little baby it's getting where she can't hang on much longer she has to step around the cubicle there are tears in her eyes fists in tiny hot balls come on stretch it we almost got it keep him talking I'll bet your cop friends would like to know where I am I can see your stinking pussy from here nothing comes from the other end of the phone except the sounds of her tears and for a second I'm sorry you asked for this you bitch you talk you won't give it to me right even though I never wanted it and told you I could have all I wanted I bet you gave it good to your cop friends did you do them one at a time or all at once oh come on baby think about it your dead body covered by flies the size of dimes black and blue and shinny feeding off your dead pussy we got it I motion to Groke let's go he's in a phone booth across the street I signal her to keep him on the line we run down the carpeted hallway down the stairs two at a time can't wait for the elevator or the Feds or the State boys in the fake light the air is still and the sky dark and fighting for light we stop dead in our tracks eyes searching can't see him where the fuck is he then I see him he's across the street in a phone booth we draw down on him and move slow and easy slow and easy the booth's dark blue a colored band on top and scratched glass stands out in the dim light he watches the two cops charge the phone booth hunched over his face bathed in a green tint from the television set he takes another shot from the bottle and lights a smoke a gray white trail snaking and crawling up the motel room wall there's a loud bang on the door and he panics spilling booze and knocking over his chair he hits the floor crawling behind the bed the door is blown off its hinges and hangs to one side police rush in crawling over the room they grab him cuff him and pull him to his feet one of the uniformed men hauls off and smashes him in the face with the butt of his riot gun he careens backwards they read him his rights you have the right to remain silent mother fucker anything you say can and will be used against you have the right to an attorney one of the cops keeps reading from a card another grabs the bag with the stolen cash he's yanked up and dragged towards the door pulling in the other direction he stops in front of the television on the screen the cops have the suspect on the ground and are cuffing him he kicks the TV off the table it teeters lands on its back with a loud explosion the tube goes dark and fizzles small sparks spitting here and there on the way out the air feels good on his cheek and nose still smarting from the gun butt to the face he tastes blood on the tip of his tongue it isn't the first time won't be the last fuck you you're all a bunch of fucking cock sucking dickheads they throw him in the back of a cage car he watches the motel fade from view his mind jumping back to the dark television tube a smile comes across his face at least he got to see the ending both the movie's and his fuck them he thinks he would have blow away four more had he had the chance five years later his soul took a one way flight propelled by cyanide gas justice met the circle complete free after all free after all.